things are not what they seem

Janine Kanzler

Printed in the U.S.A.

Published by

Fernhouse Press
Woodstock, VT 05091

ISBN 0-9759363-0-1

cover art by Hali Issente

This book is dedicated to Malia Scotch-Marmo

and

To the memory of Elizabeth Pierson Friend

things are not what they seem

1

I'm shivering from the damp leaves I'm sitting on that surround me, that scratch my neck and the exposed skin where my jeans stop and my shirt doesn't quite reach, unless I stretch it down and tuck it in. When I do, my butt feels clammy, like there's no circulation getting there. I bet it's been twenty minutes since I buried myself inside this stupid leaf pile.

Graham, who is Libby's brother, is twenty-three or something. He suggested playing sardines, and that's why I'm suffocating in here. I whispered to Libby, his sister and my best friend, "the last time I played this game was when I was ten." I didn't really want to play, so I made it seem like a babyish thing to do. But Libby whispered back, "it's fun, and Becca likes it," and that was that. Whenever Libby wants to do something and she doesn't dare say SHE wants to do it herself, she says her little sister, who's nine, likes it.

One person hides and when someone finds them they hide too, so eventually everyone is crammed into the same place together. Then, there is always one person left wandering around looking for the group. Libby and I are thirteen, her other brother William is a senior. With three or four people hiding at once, it's not easy to pick a place we can all squeeze into.

Anyway, I'm so glad I didn't go to Bermuda with my parents for this annual endless long weekend. If I were there right now, it would be exactly like last year, and the year before, and the year before that. I would be back at the Hamilton Country Club, sitting inside in the main room, across from the elderly Bridge players, while my parents slowly play thirty-six holes of golf. I've never understood why they travel so far from home to play golf with their same friends every year. Aren't they ever interested in meeting anyone new?

J.K.

I used to sit for hours in the humidity looking at the real estate sections in stacks of *Country Life* magazines, imagining that I would turn the castles that were for sale into happy homes for orphans that I would run when I got older. I sat on a leather club chair that stuck to the skin on my legs right below where my skirt stopped, the not-too-short khaki one Mom insisted I wear. I would slowly stick and unstick my skin and count how many diamond shapes there were in the gold and rose carpet all the way across the room. This year, I wouldn't be caught dead wearing anything other than jeans and a shirt.

Even though I'm thirteen now, my parents said that this year I still wouldn't be able to stay in the hotel room in the evening by myself, so I'd have to go everywhere with them. Lots of hand shaking, fake smiles (so nice to meet you, who really cares) and all I'd be wondering is when I could get to the beach. Which might not be forever, and if it did happen, I would feel like a dog that they just let off a leash as they watched me. It's weird: when I'm with them they treat me like a kindergartner, when I'm out of their sight, it seems as though they forget about me.

I started coming up to Libby's house in the late spring. That was before I came down with mononucleosis, the "kissing" disease, which was odd, because no one has ever kissed me. I've thought about kissing this guy who I love to watch dance at the country club dances. He sometimes smoothes his hair back out of his face and quickly smiles at me. But he's always standing with a circle of friends and they laugh a lot between themselves. An impossible reality, maybe a better dream.

I had to spend six weeks at the beginning of the summer lying around the house, sleeping and sleeping again, while I knew everyone else I knew was out running around, having fun. I felt like a lonely wooly bear caterpillar in its colorless cocoon. Alive, but all bound up, far from the smell of the deep pine woods where I like to walk, and the July church fair with crowds of people eating hamburgers and carrying around second hand games and clothes

that they'd bought for a quarter or two. There was nothing sponta-
neous or interesting in my life for over a month.

One thing that all that sleep made me do was grow. I slept and
I ate and I grew out of all of my clothes. So everything I wear now
is too tight, but that's better than having to go shopping with my
mom, who will try to get me to wear pink, sleeveless, collared
shirts and white Peds with pom poms on the heels.

Libby told me that every year her brothers have a huge party
on the harvest moon, with a big bonfire, and sometimes fifty
people come. She told me they get pretty wild. And I bet they're
not all wearing tasseled loafers like the guys at the Country Club
teas. More like torn jeans and bare feet. So I reminded Mom that
I was about to have mid-terms at school and that I wouldn't be
able to study at all if I was away. That was easy. She's so con-
cerned what grades I'm getting, she let me stay. Just as long as I
keep getting A's she'll give me the space I need.

Where is Libby? I wish I could see out of here, but every time I
try to make a little hole with my finger, it collapses. I hid in the
leaves because I figured she'd think of looking here right away. This
morning, we raked most of the red and yellow leaves that had fallen
off the old maple tree into the middle of her yard for Becca to jump
into. We made the pile really high, and it was fun watching Becca
fly through the air and then disappear. As she made her way out,
Libby and I would scoop more armfuls of leaves on top of her hair
and her white wool sweater that their mom had shrunk in the washing machine. Both the sweater and her red hair had a fuzziness that
made me want to push them down with the palm of my hand and
watch them spring back.

I smell a French cigarette with that sweet, thick smoke that reminds me of a cigar. Graham smokes the kind in the fat little blue
box that he keeps in the inside breast pocket of his old tweed jacket.
I know the smell because last summer when my parents and I were
in Paris, the smell was always in the air. Graham wears that jacket no

matter what the weather, or the occasion. It's too big for him, but he thinks he's really cool the way he moves it back off his shoulders and at the same time, shakes and smoothes his long blonde hair. He's probably got the butt hanging out of his mouth right now while he ties his boot. Then he'll take a few short puffs so it's only half way smoked, and stamp on it. Mr. Predictable. If he gets any closer, I'll gag. At last, I can hear his footsteps crunching away from here, though the smell lingers behind him.

I just sucked a piece of leaf into my nostril and I think I'm going to sneeze. If I do, it will give me away. If I rub the area between my upper lip and my nostril, as I learned in some Nancy Drew book years ago, it will stop the feeling. It worked, and just in time because I hear some coughs and the sound of shuffling getting closer and closer.

I'm pretty sure it's Libby's mom—she's a night nurse for an elderly man with emphysema and a hip problem. She goes to work at 8pm and comes home at 7am, and takes a long nap in the afternoon. Her name is Catherine. Everyone calls her that, even Libby and Becca. I can't imagine calling my mother by her first name, or any of her friends. Although we do call our teachers by their first names. I can never actually say "Catherine," though I've come to think it. She really doesn't seem like a mother, she seems like a gray haired, older sibling of Libby's who hasn't really figured out how to manage the house or her family yet.

She says that she quit smoking at the beginning of the summer. How is it that smokers never realize that their breath, their hair, and especially their clothes smell like smoke? There's that cough again, and it sounds like a sea lion barking, deep from the lungs, and I heard it at the kitchen table this morning. When I first came over to Libby's house four months ago, I believed her mom when she said she needed more throat lozenges for her endless cold. But I know better now.

Off she goes, shuffling slowly through the leaves, probably wearing those ratty gray slippers that have dry egg yolk on them, not at all like the black silk Chinese scuffs with the pointed toes that my mother wears. Back to reading one of her many copies of *Prevention* magazine scattered around the house. She always announces facts from them, like "rosemary helps your memory." Then, there's an unusual flurry of cooking and rosemary is the featured ingredient in everything the family eats: rosemary chicken, rosemary bread and rosemary candy, which was particularly disgusting. If she wasn't cooking, then she'd just chew on the rosemary stem straight from the newly bought plant. The next week, she'd read an article about garlic being good for the heart, and the rosemary disappears and everything includes garlic. Once it was watercress, another time cashews.

The rest of the time everyone eats mostly white bread with American cheese slices and canned tomato soup. I hope she doesn't drop her cigarette butt on the leaf pile. Headlines: "Sardines Player Never Found," until the spring maybe, when Libby's little mutt, Blackie, would casually drop a large charred bone on the front steps. Good job, Blackie, what a big bone!

All fall I've been arranging it so that my mother never has to drop me off at Libby's. I get a ride from Libby's mom, or sometimes Graham or William, and a couple of times I've ridden my bike all three and a half miles uphill. My mom was named chairperson of the Autumn Tea at the country club so she spends a lot of time on the phone, planning the table decorations and the trophies. Also, she's busy playing tennis or paddle tennis, so she's happy not to have another thing to do. Actually, most of the time when I'm up here, I say that I'm at the library studying or that I'm going for a walk or a bike ride.

My dad is always busy running his real estate office. He works late, and when he does get home he just wants to have a gin and tonic and read the paper, undisturbed. The one thing we do together is build telescopes and belong to an astronomy club. Once, when he and I were coming out of the hardware store after buying a screw for our scope's tripod, he muttered, "creep" when we saw Graham walking on the other side of the street. Something stopped me from asking him how he knew him, and I knew I wouldn't be asking him to give me a ride up to Libby's house. Ever.

If Mom ever saw this place she'd never let me come back. The blue van without wheels in the yard, the old iron radiators rusting on the front porch, the milking shed where the roof is collapsing. Inside it there are bags of garbage stacked on top of each other, surrounded by the hum of giant blue-bodied flies.

Every time I sit on the old plaid couch that's been shredded by generations of house cats, I think of how Mom's nose would wrinkle as though she smelled something bad. I see her saying, "Cynthia, that couch is offensive." She spent six weeks choosing the fabric for the sofa in our living room at home, and no one is allowed to eat or drink anywhere near it. And that's just one thing she'd hate.

Libby's parents wouldn't be at the top of her approval list, either. Her father's never here. I've seen him four or five times ever since I've known Libby. And he dresses just the opposite way from my dad. Dad always wears a blue sport coat and striped tie, and Mark, yes same first-name business with Libby's dad, wears a plaid button down shirt with an ink stain on the bottom of the breast pocket and the same corduroy pants that are worn at the knees. When he is here, he yells at everyone.

The only time he's sort of nice is when he has three or four beers at lunchtime. Sometimes he pulls Libby's and my ear lobes gently and smiles at us, telling us that we're growing up too fast. A few times he's done it to me when I've been by myself on the stairs or when I've been running out the door. At first I liked when he did it, now I avoid him.

Everything is always the same at my house. The house is always perfectly tidy. Thanks to our cleaning lady that cleans twice a week even though there's nothing to clean up. I always know exactly when everything will happen and how everyone will act. It's completely boring. At Libby's I'm surprised at least half the time.

Someone else is coming. The leaves are crunching underfoot and there's no shuffling or coughing. If it were Libby or Becca, there would definitely be shuffling. They love hearing the swishing noise so much, and if it were Graham coming back, there'd be no noise at all. Graham loves to hide and sneak up on us, even when we're not playing a game, always proving he can outsmart us. So, it must be William.

Like me, William didn't seem too excited about playing sardines. When Graham brought it up, he suggested we play soccer instead in the hayfield that's just been cut, that it would help Becca out because she's on her third-grade team.

Libby said, "You never want to play sardines," and William just looked at her and shrugged. Graham said, "There are too many woodchuck holes for soccer and we might twist our ankle in one of them." That didn't make any sense, and we all knew it because all the holes are in the hillside where we wouldn't be playing.

Graham always gets his way over William, which is weird because William is so much smarter. William won the high school physics prize last spring for building the strongest bridge out of straws, whereas Graham went to college for two months, then dropped out, and hasn't done anything except odd painting jobs around town.

I'm not sure if I should give William a clue that I'm here. I really want Libby to find me first. At least he's wearing a shirt today. All summer and fall I've been looking at his ribs and his "outie" belly button. He's so skinny, but he's got really strong arms. I love watching him haying, lifting all of the bales onto the back of the truck. When he gets thirsty from the work, he opens up a carton of orange juice that would last all week at my house with my parents and me drinking it, and he gulps it down in minutes.

I don't really think I want him in here with me, alone. I can't hear him any more, so either he's just standing there, or he's gone.

It is so freaking cold in here. Where is she? Yes! No shuffling this time, just fast crunching, right towards me.

"Cynthia, are you in there?" Libby is breathing hard.

"Yes, stupid."

She slowly burrows in next to me, waking up the smell of leaves and I can finally really move. Like a blind mole, she bumps her head into my stomach and I smell the herbal shampoo that she washes her hair with every morning. I re-direct her and position her so that she's curled up with the back of her sweater towards my chest. Then, I hold onto her, around her stomach, for warmth, because she is very warm. We are like one person, not two, inside the pile.

"If we are close together there is less chance anyone will guess we're in here," I tell her. I tell myself. I hold my hands around her stomach and squeeze her gently. She pats my hands and turns her head back a little so that our cheeks just barely touch, hers warm, mine cold. We have each other for a few seconds of time. I'm very happy that I didn't go with my parents. In some ways it would be nice if I never had to go home.

"We are little squirrels," I say.

"Let's hibernate like this all winter," she says and she couldn't have said anything better. I close my eyes and breathe in the smell of her and the leaves and I'm so relaxed, far away from the rest of my life. Close to my friend.

2

"Is it raining or what?" Libby asks. Her warm breath touches my cheek and tickles me a little down my neck, making me shiver. I hear the water on top of us too, and it doesn't sound like the gentle pattering that begins a rainstorm. It's a rush of water, a steady stream that is being purposely directed here and there. Obviously, we're being hosed, and we're trapped.

"Jerks," I murmur. I'm too cozy and I don't want it to end. Too bad for me. "I'll count to three, then we can bolt out of here in different directions, or we can run together straight down the hill towards the pond. The hose isn't all that long so we can get out of his range quickly." I said "his," but we both know who I mean. William and Becca might be there, but their instigator has to be Graham.

I feel Libby nod, but I'm not sure what the nod means. I give her a gentle push away from me as I say, "Three." My breath comes back at me off her hair and the warm, not so pleasant smell of it surprises me. It reminds me of the insides of my body, like my tongue, and my gums that bled when I flossed them this morning. Graham walked into the bathroom when I was in there and brushed his teeth while watching me. The thought stops me, but now I realize Libby is already following my directions and is out of the pile. I can hear her and Becca screaming and Graham roaring and yelping with satisfaction.

I crawl out fast on my hands and knees into the warm light and the brightness of the sun surprises me. I stand up into a run, squinting, my eyes open just enough that I can see where I'm headed downhill. I keep going past the point where I think the tightest, furthest stretch of the hose is, and I hear more shouting. As I get to the bottom where the lawn ends and the sumac and the brown furry spikes of the cattails grow, right before the pond begins, I stop.

Looking back up the hill, I shade my eyes with my hand to see if I can see anyone under the maple tree, in the yard, or on the farmhouse's porch.

I'm waiting to see if anyone appears, but there seems to be no one around. I think if I slowly walk back up the hill, then they won't be able to ambush me. Dark clouds cross in front of the sun and a cold wind makes the dead leaves on the trees and the brown seedy ferns next to the lawn rustle. I walk by the pile of shiny, wet leaves and the abandoned hose that has a slow trickle of water escaping from it into the grass.

At the porch, I step up the peeling dark green steps that show red paint underneath and wonder how it's possible they look like that when Graham and some of his friends painted the steps and the porch at the beginning of the summer. There are the black rubber barn boots Becca always wears covered in wet grass and leaves and a lot of wet bare footprints. They must be inside. I kick off my leather sandals next to them.

I push open the screen door, but forget to hold it and it slams behind me, loud in the silence of the narrow hallway. I think I see something move swiftly across the landing at the top of the stairs, but when I look hard, nothing is there. I open the door to the kitchen and Libby and Becca are sitting at the kitchen table as close to each other as they can get. They look at me; their eyes big like frightened fawns.

"Mom got some phone call and she started screaming at Graham about not showing up for an appointment and then he screamed at her something about how he's not the only person who says he going to be one place and then is in another, and then he threw the hose at her and she threw her coffee mug at him. So Libby was lucky, Graham only sprayed her once." I've never heard Becca speak so much at once.

"Oh" is all I can manage. I look at Libby, but she looks away when she sees my questioning eyes. I don't know whether or not to keep standing or sit down with them. The silence is broken by heavy footsteps and the screen door slams.

"Okay, let's not let Mom ruin everything again." Graham says even louder than usual. His tan work boots are spreading dirt and little clumps of wet leaves all over the kitchen floor. "Smile," he says to Libby, as he pulls a chair away from the table. The smell of his sweat, moldy shirt and cigarettes, hangs in the air from where he passed by me. He tips the chair onto its back legs, an act that is a capital offense in my house, and rocks it with his dirty boots, one hand on the edge of the table for support. There's some kind of black sludge pushed deep under his nails that overflows past his nails at the top. I think of my dad's nails, clean and filed. It looks like Graham just had a fingerprint taken of his whole hand.

"What are you looking at?" he says bringing his chair down hard. I look at Libby because I think she might say something to distract him, but she's staring at the table, definitely still not speaking.

"Nothing," I say, brilliantly. In one move he pushes himself off his chair and kneels in front of me, takes my hand, and turns it over gently so my palm is face up.

"Has anyone ever read your palm, Cynthia?" He studies my palm; turning it a little from side to side in his dark, warm hand. Somehow, it doesn't seem like my hand is in his. My hand seems very far away. I shake my head no, though it isn't true, because one time when I was at a county fair a woman with too much dark purple eye shadow read my palm and told me that I wouldn't live past twenty-one. I ran away from her as fast as I could.

"It looks as though you'll have a long life, that you'll marry once and you'll have two children. This line," he says as he slowly presses his finger horizontally across my hand, "is proof that you tend to procrastinate." Since I've just figured this fact out for myself in the last two weeks, I'm amazed to find that the truth is so obvious every time I open my hand. "And these little lines here," he says pushing down hard with his thumb on the side of my hand, "they mean you'll have a lot of lovers." I pull my hand away quickly and he laughs. "It's all right, Cynthia. Nothing you can do about it."

We hear the front door shut softly.

"Man, it is wet out there!" William says as he appears in the doorway. His brown, usually thick and wavy hair looks black, and it's plastered flat to his head. Water is dripping down the side of his face, which looks rosy and freckled and happy. I can feel the girls relax. Until now, I haven't even noticed that it's raining very hard, blowing sideways inside the porch. A big clap of thunder rattles the windows a little.

"I'm scared," Becca whimpers.

"I'm not." Libby gets up from her chair and walks by me, tapping me on the shoulder, as she heads for the door. "Come on." I look at her to see if I can get a reading from her face, some hint of what she might be up to, but all I see is determination. I jump up, thrust my hands into my front jeans' pockets and give a skip to get out of there fast.

The rain is bouncing off the steps with a sound like sleet, but Libby doesn't stop. She keeps going right down the steps, taking off her sweater over her head, pausing only to fling it back up onto the porch. I watch as she twirls round and round, her arms straight out like wings, faster and faster. She leans her neck back and the rain pelts her face and her bare arms. In a few seconds her dry blonde hair is transformed and looks just like William's, except that it's down to her waist, draping over her shoulders, clinging to her body in thick wet strands. She smiles, so different from the way she looked at the kitchen table. She staggers a bit and I can tell she's dizzy, twirling into the leaf pile we'd been hiding in. I watch as she slips and falls down. She lies on her back, arched over the top of the pile, laughing. Then, she slowly props herself up on her elbows and tries to open her eyes, but it's raining too hard. There's a little rumble of thunder in the distance.

"Cynthia, get over here," and I realize that I've been watching her for a while. I'd been afraid to go out while the thunder was right overhead, but now the storm seems to be moving off and the rain's letting up a little bit. My parents have told me a million times how dangerous it is to be outside when it's thundering and lightening, usually as we sit in the screened-in deck of the country club, watching golfers scurry for cover as sheets of rain pass over the course.

I find myself on the porch steps, running towards her. She stands up with two hands full of wet leaves and starts to chase me. Even though she's smaller than I am, she's a faster runner, and wound up, crazy, so she catches me in no time. She jumps onto my back and hangs from my neck; the wet leaves in her hands tickling me. I can't hold her, so I fall down and she sits on my back, pinning me. As I twist around, she crams all the leaves she can down my shirt.

"AHHHHHH!" I hear myself scream. I'm starting to feel a little crazy too, and I feel her relax, so I twist as hard as I can, wrapping my legs around hers, and she falls on her back. My turn to sit on her, pin her arms above her head and bounce on her stomach just a little.

I try to think of more ways to torture her. But she says, "Let's go swimming." I leap off her and run so fast my legs feel like they can't keep up with themselves, down the hill to the pond. I slow down to consider what clothes I'll take off, but Libby goes right in with her blue jeans and tee shirt on. I scream a war cry and run into the water with high kicks, splashing as much as I can. I stop and put my arms at my side and fall, a stiff body flop, into the water. My clothes become heavy and I feel pulled down to the bottom by their weight. Libby is swimming out into the middle of the pond concentrating very hard on her breaststroke, and just as I'm wondering how she can swim so well with her pants on, something moves against my ankles and through the murky brown water I can see her blue jeans.

"I think you lost something," I scream at her through the rain, which is heavy again. I try to hold up the jeans, but they feel like they weigh at least thirty pounds. She's smiling at me as she treads water and blows bubbles just below the surface. I'm freezing, so I sit

13

down quickly up to my neck on the sandy bottom in the warmth of the pond. Yesterday I put my fingers in the water and it felt icy to me, and now I am using it like a blanket to keep warm.

She swims closer like a crocodile with her eyes just above the water and pulls herself with her hands along the bottom, so her body floats at the top. She opens her lips slightly and I see her teeth clenched tight, the gap between her front teeth filled with the tip of her tongue. Before I figure out what she's doing, she shoots an arc of water all over my face.

"You got me all wet!" I joke and splash her in the face.

She splashes me back. When she pauses for a moment, I see that she's shaking beyond control and her skin looks gray, her lips bluish purple.

"Your lips are really purple," she says through her convulsions.

"Same with yours. Are you going to try to put these on?" I hold up the jeans so they are half out of the water. She takes them out of my hands and twists one of the legs so that the water pours out of them at the same time the rain gently patters down. I stand up and look at my own jeans that are suctioned to my legs and consider taking them off. Libby stands up out of the water and her legs look so white and boney and her skin is covered with goose bumps. I think I'll keep my pants on.

"Hot bath," she chatters, as she drags her pants through the sand and wet grass. I walk behind her, my pants squishing and squeaking, and somehow the waist has shrunk.

"Nice panties," I say. She must notice the way they cling to her, stretched way beyond their normal shape because she laughs and sticks out her skinny butt and waves it, crying "WA WA WA." She's laughing so much that she falls to the ground. She looks quickly up towards the house, so I do too. Graham's standing a little behind one of the posts that holds up the porch roof. He's so still that I'm not really sure it's him.

As I watch him, he turns his head a little. He reminds me of the big red-tailed hawk that sometimes sits in my grandmother's old oak tree, waiting for a chipmunk, or a mole, or a mouse. One moment the hawk looks like part of the limbs of the tree and the next moment, he swoops down and then up with his snack. Graham must see me looking, because without turning his back, he steps behind the post and the front door opens and shuts.

"He was watching you, you know," Libby says.

"Don't make me sick," I growl. "He's probably just trying to figure out when we're coming back so we can keep playing."

"Yeah, right," Libby mumbles quickly. "I'm putting a skirt on."

She walks over to the picnic table where a plastic red checked tablecloth has been sitting since the first spring picnic. Little puddles filled with leaves and bugs weigh it down here and there. She pulls it off in a flourish and it hangs in her hand to the ground. She tries to shake it out as you do a sheet, before you fold it, and the rotting debris splatters my body.

"Oh thank you SO much," I say. The cloth is stiff, but she manages to wrap it around herself in an ugly sarong.

"First person to the porch gets the bath first." Libby's already running, pushing her chicken legs, which occasionally show through a slit in the back, up the hill. There is no point humiliating myself by trying to beat her when there is no way I can. So, I saunter a bit, trying to make it look like it's cool to be slow. The rain has stopped, so I pause and look up at the clouds, pretending to identify them, though the whole sky is gray. I shiver, it's freezing and I wonder when the first snowfall will be, and if Graham packs ice into his snowballs.

15

3

Looking toward the house, I see Libby walking through the front door. The race is over and I don't want to miss any reactions there might be to her attractive outfit, so I run as fast as I can up the hill. When I get to the top of the steps, I hear lots of laughing.

"Well, if it ain't Miss America," Graham's friend Caleb says. I walk into the kitchen where Libby's family and Caleb are looking at her. Caleb is sitting next to Graham and they're both hand-rolling cigarettes, which they always claim is made out of tobacco, on the kitchen table. It seems to be their favorite hobby. William's holding a calculus book. Libby's mother is braiding Becca's hair, brushing it out with a brush that doesn't have half of its plastic bristles. I immediately feel in the spotlight, since everyone's staring at me too, and terrible because I'm dripping water all over the floor. If I run up the stairs to change, it means more drips all over the house. If my parents saw me like this, they would completely flip out.

"You girls had better dry off your hair," Libby's mother says. That's random, I think. What about the rest of our bodies?

"I've got a better idea," Libby says. "Let's suck it dry." We both grab up some ends of our own hair and suck it, making great wet noises. It's surprising how truly drenched my hair is, enough for a real drink. It tastes of pond water and shampoo.

"Pretty weird," says Caleb, shaking his head, tapping the cigarette on the table. Actually, I think Caleb is pretty weird. He's missing three of his front teeth and half of his middle finger. He has some explanation of a tractor tipping over on him when he was eight. Where he lives there's always deerskins drying on a tall wooden rack in the yard. It looks like the same ones year round. He likes to talk about drinking shots of Wild Turkey with maple syrup. All of his five siblings squeeze into the front of their rusty yellow pick-up, and you can hear it coming down the dirt driveway before it arrives at Libby's house. He lost his license two weeks after he got it, in that truck. The sheriff happened to pass by him when he was driving at night on the back road headed to a pig roast. On further inspection, the sheriff found two loaded, unlicensed guns, and a deer carcass jacked out of season next to one of Caleb's brothers passed out drunk in the bed of the truck. Caleb refused to take a breath test to find out his blood alcohol level and he kicked and swore at the sheriff. Really smart, Caleb.

Graham's looking at me, this time at my shirt. I look down to see what he's looking at, and it's soaking wet and my nipples look big and hard through it. Libby was smarter than I thought to put the tablecloth on. I look at Graham, trying to make him look at me in the face, and he immediately looks away.

"Why don't you girls go and dry off or change or something, and then we'll play one more game of sardines," he says in a huskier, authoritative voice than he usually uses.

"Yes sir," I say smiling at Libby.

"I only want to play if I can stay with Libby or William," whines Becca as her mother winds the elastic around the end of her second tight braid. "I get too scared looking for everyone by myself, and I hate being last."

"You can stay with me," William says, walking over and putting his arm around her. "I say this last time, whoever hides, has to hide inside. It's too wet out."

"Libby has to hide because she found Cynthia first," Graham says.

"You know it's the last person to find the person who was hiding who gets to be it," William says.

"Yeah, you're right, except there wasn't really a last person last time, because we all found them at once." Graham pauses. "And besides, Libby hasn't been it yet."

I notice Libby's mother tapping her sweater pocket as she stands up and heads for the door. Everyone moves around without announcement here, another difference from my house. At home it's considered impolite to just go and do something without saying what you're doing and when you might return. Even if you're just going to the bathroom.

"Come on," I hear Libby saying through my thoughts. "And don't worry about the floor." She knows me well and she's been to my house. She's already dripping up the wooden stairs. I hold onto the banister so that I won't slip in her tracks.

"Don't take too long," Graham shouts after us.

"Let's take a bath later," Libby says as she turns into her room at the top of the stairs. Actually, the room she shares with Becca. The two of them painted it bright purple, which is always a shock no matter how many times I go in there. Posters of kittens and Switzerland (though no one in the family has ever been there) are taped to the wall. I'm not allowed to hang posters in my room, or anything I'd like, for that matter. Mom chose some local artist's work, colorful woodprints of cows and hills and barns that have hung there since I was born.

"I don't know if my pants will fit you," Libby says, squeaking open the drawer to the dresser. It's on Becca's side of the bed and on the top of it is her used Band-Aids, bloodied side up, in a little row. I don't know why, but she likes looking at them, and gets mad if Libby says they should be thrown out.

"I think I'll see if there are any towels in the bathroom," I announce through my shivers.

"There are clean ones in the cupboard in there," she says, continuing to pull stuff out of the drawer, piling it on the floor.

I drip across the little hallway to the bathroom that the whole family shares. I shut the door and slowly tug my jeans off in a see saw motion and throw them and my underpants into the old fashioned tub. Then my shirt and my bra. Brownish water and sand run slowly down the middle of the bathtub into the drain. I hadn't realized there was so much dirt in everything. I like the tub with its old claw feet.

There's a shower attached to the faucets by a rusty pipe that everyone complains about because it's too short, and Libby's brothers can't get underneath it and the water comes out in a trickle. If anyone turns on a faucet anywhere else in the house while it's going, the person showering gets a blast of freezing, or worse, scalding water. There's a baby blue shower curtain, made out of plastic that's really thick. It has cracks in it and black mold creeping up from the bottom. I stare at the curtain thinking I might lock the door and take a bath despite everyone else's desire to keep playing sardines, but then I would have to touch that curtain because it is on the inside of the tub.

I open the cupboard door and there are lots of towels, all different sizes and colors crammed onto a couple of shelves. They are sort of folded, like I fold my napkins after eating. There are colored ones in front and white ones stuffed in back. I take out a lime green one and unfold it. It's the size of a bath mat, but not thick like one. The ends of it are threadbare. I hold it to my nose and it smells moldy. I drop it on the linoleum and step on it and take out a cherry red towel. I put it to my nose and it smells too soapy and feels sort of slippery. It's incredibly stiff and I try to dry my body with it, but it reminds me more of one of my mother's scratchy loofah sponges than a towel. I rub it on my hair, but there's no way that it's going to absorb any water, so I fold it over the side of the tub. I don't want to waste towels; a high crime at my house, so I think someone can use it as a mat. If I take one of the white ones in back, I might have more luck. I reach in and pull a grayish white one out that is as thin as a dishtowel, but it doesn't smell or feel weird, it's just dusty. It actually works to dry my hair, so I towel myself off and wrap it like a sarong around me. Since the white one was successful, I think I'll choose one like it for Libby. I slide my hand past the towels in front and slowly pull a big whitish one toward me. As I do, I drag with it mouse turds that fall and scatter like pebbles around my bare feet. The floor is so dirty already with little dust balls made of cat hair and God knows what else, that the turds immediately become part of the landscape.

"What are you doing in there? I'm freezing!" I open the door to find Libby completely naked, so I throw the towel at her.

"Don't you have a robe?"

"I don't know where it is."

"Show off."

I look at her body as she wraps the towel around her. She can't quite get the tightness she wants so she opens it and closes it, trying to make it right. Her breasts look so different from mine, smaller, with dark nipples. And she has a scar where her appendix came out when she was Becca's age. I follow her back into her room.

"The only pants I think will fit you are jeans that used to be William's. They're too small for him and too big for me." She holds them up.

"You got a belt?" I ask.

She hands me a crocheted one with lots of bright colors, the kind without a buckle, with metal hoops you thread the belt through. Everything looks way too big on me, but I like the idea that I'll be wearing something that used to be William's.

"And here's one of my turtlenecks."

It doesn't matter to me whether I wear underwear or not and I don't want to ask for it, so I pull the turtleneck over my head. It's a bit tight, but it smells clean and it's soft and warm. I step into the dark hole that's the waist of William's blue jeans. I don't need to unbutton them or unzip them they're so big. I put the belt in the loops and pull it tight so there are at least nine inches of left over belt hanging down. I look down at myself and for some reason, I feel great. Libby's finished dressing, too, and she's looking into the little unframed mirror above her dresser, brushing out her hair. I never like to look in that mirror because it makes my face look long and ugly, so I stand away from it.

"Almost ready?" I say.

She nods and I feel warm and safe, and ready for some more fun.

4

"Christ, we'd almost given up on you," Caleb says, taking a drag off his cigarette. So attractive, the way he squints through the cloud of smoke in front of his face. Everyone's staring at us. I can't look back at them, not for long, anyway.

"Those jeans look a lot better on you than they ever did on me," William says, smiling.

"So, Libby's going to hide?" Becca asks in her squeaky high, take-care-of-me voice. Her long braids and round face remind me of Heidi.

"We'll all stand on the front porch to count, so you'll have the whole house to hide in," Graham says.

"Count to thirty," says Libby. We always count to twenty.

"Twenty," we say.

"Twenty-five, because the house is harder."

"No it isn't," William says.

"Give her twenty-five," I say, firmly.

Graham looks at me and smiles nicely and stretches his arms out above his head. "O.K., twenty-five," he says. Since he is usually so weird, I never feel comfortable when he's agreeable.

We walk out onto the porch and surprisingly Caleb shuffles along with us. William shuts the door.

"No peeking in the windows, especially you, Becca," he says.

"But what happens if she hides in the basement?"

I'd have to agree with her on that one. The one time I'd been down there to help Libby's mom carry up the laundry, which hadn't been done for weeks, half the dirt floor was under water and it smelled muddy, like a river after a rainstorm. There was the noise of a sump pump going. I knew, because we have one in our basement that works. This one sounded a little weird, though, and obviously wasn't working, so I kept thinking that if my foot touched the water, I'd be electrocuted. There were a couple of boards laid between the bottom of the stairs and the washing machine and dryer, which were up on concrete blocks.

"Twelve, thirteen," I hear them counting and mouth along, but I'm remembering how when Libby's mother stepped on one of those boards, it submerged for a moment and I'd held my breath, waiting to see if she'd be zapped. Nothing happened except that a little wave started lapping at the metal support poles holding up the crossbeams.

As I watched the wave, I noticed that something was floating in the darkness beside it. Libby's mother pulled the clothes out and put them on top of the rusty dryer, and I strained my eyes to see. Immediately I wished I hadn't. The shape of the head, and that tail. A rat. A big one, swimming about ten feet away.

"Don't want to get those new sneakers wet?" Libby's mother had asked, oblivious.

"Not really," I mumbled, looking sideways at the rat. I didn't know how to tell her it was there without being impolite. The rat had made a little splash then with its tail, and Libby's mother turned and looked right at its horrible wet fur. Without a word, she turned back for more clothes and piled them on top of my outstretched arms.

"You're not counting, Cynthia," I hear Becca say. They're already up to twenty-three.

"Ready or not, here we come," shouts William, opening the door. I look at Caleb. Has anyone explained to him how to play? I'm not going to. I walk in and listen intently for any last minute shuffling or a door closing, but no such luck, especially because everyone else is making so much noise. Caleb walks into the kitchen, sits down at the table and pulls out a tobacco pouch and a pack of rolling papers. I guess he isn't playing.

Now where would Libby go? If she wants to be truly rotten, she'll go into the basement, but I know she hates it down there too, so it won't be my first stop. I'm alone in the hallway and realize they've all disappeared. Maybe they've found her already. Am I the last one? I doubt it. If she can, she might pick a spot I know about that no one else will think of. Maybe up in her room. In the closet or even under the bed. I try to picture everyone squeezed together under her bed.

I make my way as quietly as I can up the stairs, skipping the third step from the top that always creaks. If she is in her room, I don't want anyone else to know I'm there. No one is in the hallway, so I push open her door and then close it, not quite shut behind me. From the moment I step in I sense she isn't there, but I think maybe I might be wrong, so I get down on my hands and knees and look under the bed. No, not there. Just huge dust balls. I get up and go over to the walk-in closet Libby shares with Becca. I swing the door open, quickly, dramatically, so I can surprise her before she surprises me, but the only thing that rushes towards me is the damp air of the empty closet. I push back the hanging clothes, just in case, but there's no one there. Maybe this will be my hiding spot when I'm it.

Now let's get serious. Where is she? Libby's father tore down an old shed in the spring, and added a family room to the back of the house. He did it because Graham and William always have tons of friends over and they want to play music and party, and, besides, he's in the construction business and he said it would increase the value of the house when it gets sold. Libby says he's renovated every house they've lived in, most of them in Connecticut. Maybe that's where he got the idea for the new room, because it doesn't look like the rest of this house at all. It's huge, and her father still hasn't completed the work on the floor, which is just unfinished plywood. The ceiling is really high and at the top of the wall there's a stained glass window in the shape of a rainbow. Some friend of theirs designed the glass and put it in because they owed Libby's father money. It's a nice idea, but the colors look wrong—orange next to pink, next to gray.

In the room there's a loft that Graham and William's friends sleep in. Libby and I never want to go up there because it's pretty dark and you have to climb a narrow ladder attached to the wall, and you can't put your foot all the way on top of the rung because the wall stops your foot. The one time I climbed to the top, it smelled of pee, like I've smelled in New York City in the summer. It drove me back down. From the family room floor, you can see dark green beer bottles and balled up plaid shirts that stay there week after week. It's definitely older brother territory. It's possible Libby might go up there, but I really doubt it.

I head back downstairs, avoiding the noisy step again. I still can't hear any sounds and I begin to think I'm the last one to find her. I glance into the kitchen, and Caleb's still there, this time with his back to me, his dirty sneakers on the table. Thank God he can't see me, because I'm sure he'd say something like, "You ain't found them yet, Cynthia?" and then everyone would know where I'm looking, and I want to find Libby myself.

I walk into the little hallway that leads to the family room and all the lights are off. It's late afternoon and it's pretty dark. I don't like the idea of having to walk in there by myself. There's no avoiding the creaking of the plywood, it's arched up in too many places, put in green, in a hurry, like they did on the pavilion at my parents' tennis club last summer. There's a closet on the left-hand side where I've seen Libby's mother take out large packs of paper towels and toilet paper. I start to walk by it and a chill runs through me. I guess my hair is still pretty wet. I hear a noise in the closet. I listen again and there's definitely a sound in there, breathing or something. I look both ways to make sure no one's watching me, now that I've found her. I slowly open the door and I can't see a thing.

"Libby?" I whisper. There's no answer. "Libby?" I shut the door softly behind me. I feel ahead with my arms, like in blind man's bluff and then I smell the moldy clothes. Right then, he starts tickling me under my arms. I jerk forward, trying to stifle my giggling.

"Quit it!" I gasp.

"Your girlfriend isn't here," Graham says.

24

Oh great, I think.

"Your hair's still wet," he says massaging the back of my head quickly in the dark. He starts tickling me again and this time I fall forward onto him, not knowing where he is, where the wall is. I look for some light coming from outside the door so I can get back to it, get out of here, keep looking for Libby.

He stops tickling me under my arms and slides his hands down past my elbows to my wrists. He makes his hands like bracelets around them.

"You have the skinniest wrists of anyone I've ever seen." He takes my fingers in between his fingers and squeezes them softly. "We'll look for her in a minute," he says. I try to twist my hands out of his, but I can't. Dad used to play a game with me when I was younger where he would squeeze my fingers in his, to show me how strong he was. Then he would say, "I'm the boss applesauce."

Graham puts his arms at my sides and turns me around slowly so that my back is up against the wall. He kisses me gently around the outsides of my mouth, pretty kisses, like I give my mother's cat on her forehead and ears sometimes. And then, with his tongue, strong and sharp, he pierces through my lips. He lets go my hands and holds my shoulders, kissing me harder. He shudders and pulls his body away from mine, still kissing me, but now little kisses all over my cheeks and forehead.

"Where did you learn to do that?" he says, attempting to ruffle my wet head. I'm not sure what I've done.

"Are you there, Libby?" Becca finds the light switch on the outside of the door I so cleverly missed when I came in here, a hundred, thousand years ago. "What are you guys doing?" She looks past us to the back of the closet. "Is Libby behind the boxes?"

"Shhhh!" Graham says. "We thought we heard someone in here, but we were wrong."

"We" thought "we" heard someone in here? Becca is looking at me, but I can't speak. I can barely look at her.

25

"You're not playing the game right, Cynthia," she whispers loudly. Believe me Becca, I want to play the game right: I want to find Libby, and end the game. Then I want to watch a TV show, eat dinner, and go to bed. And sleep late. Is it tomorrow my parents are coming back? No tomorrow is Saturday, and they won't be back until Tuesday, late on Tuesday.

"I want to look for Libby by myself," I say, not looking directly at anyone. I walk slowly out of the closet, most of me wanting to run faster than I've ever run in my life. Most of me. Another part wants a very, very, very little more.

I can't think where she might be. I can't think. I feel like I don't know the house, where anything is. Like waking up in my own bed after traveling with my parents back from a trip, thinking I'm back at the hotel or in some mixture of my bed and the bed on the trip. A room in a dream, and now I'm in a house in a dream. A good dream and a bad dream. I go out into the hallway and sit on the stairs and Graham walks by.

"Maybe I'll see you later," he says quietly. I start to look up at him, then stop. I can't figure out what he means. Of course he will see me later, I'm spending the night. I keep my head down, picking at my toenails and he walks away.

Libby must be in the livingroom, but where? I push my body off the stairs and go down there. I'm tired of this now. I want to find her. "Libby?" I'm asking for a clue from her. She squeaks like a baby duck. I make the same noise. There's a little pause and then, clearly, from behind the old couch comes the answer. I leap across the room, and in the dark space between the couch and the wall is my friend.

"You certainly took your time," she says.

"Well, I'm here now." There isn't much room and I can't quite imagine how she thinks two more people are going to cram in with us behind there. I sit with my legs pulled close to my chest, which gives me more room. As I bring my legs up, I remember him kissing

26

me. Out of nowhere I feel his mouth on my mouth, and his tongue. I lean to the side and rest my head on Libby's shoulder.

"You tired?" she interrupts my drifting.

"Yeah," I say, but I really don't know what I am. The words tired, or sad or happy or homesick, (I can't believe I thought of homesick) are not describing how I feel. Maybe quiet, like I don't want to talk and I don't want anyone talking to me. Except Libby.

"I heard Caleb calling someone on the phone, talking to them about the party," Libby whispers. Until a few minutes ago, this would have been good news.

At the beginning of the summer we'd watched silhouettes of Graham and different friends go down to the pond and get high, the sweet smell of the pot drifting over us as we sat in the hayfield above them, under the stars. We loved looking at the little ember of the joint as it passed between them, listening to the silence broken only by the frogs calling quickly to each other, and occasional bursts of infectious giggling. But now I want to be inside, in Libby's room, deep in my sleeping bag, sleeping.

"I feel sort of sick or something," I manage to say. I think about being outside in the cold, all wet. Maybe there is something to my mother's warnings about not getting cold and wet. Maybe you really can get sick. Maybe I should call our housekeeper, and tell her I need to get some more clothes, and then maybe I should stay home because I don't want anyone else to catch my cold or whatever I'm getting.

"After they find us, we can take baths," Libby says. "Bubble baths." She knows how I love bubble baths. We like to turn on the faucets as hard as we can, twist off the top of the bubble bath gook and pour it into the flow. No capfuls for us. We smile at each other.

"I hear you!" shouts Becca, rupturing the quiet. I don't care if she screams, though, because everyone will know where we are and this stupid game can finally be over with. She climbs up over the top of the couch and Libby reaches up to guide her down beside us.

"First you hide all by yourself with Graham and now you're all by yourself with Libby," she reports. Libby looks at me. There's too much to explain and I can't explain it now with Becca here, and I can't explain it anyway.

"Well, I got it right this time," I say shrugging, smiling. Then I look up and roll my eyes like "she's so stupid and she doesn't know what she's talking about and I'll explain it later and it's nothing anyway." One of those looks. Libby gets it, but I can tell she's still interested because she smiles back acknowledging the message, but the curiosity hasn't gone from her eyes.

Suddenly it's darker and we all look up at the same time. William is leaning over the top of the couch, his arms outstretched, his hands open, Frankenstein style.

"Hurry up and get over here before Graham sees you," Libby says. He walks around the side of the couch and pushes it forward so there'll be enough room for him. As he sits down, we hear voices rising from the kitchen.

"Did I hear you ask Caleb to pick up the kegs for the party tonight?" Libby's mother does not sound happy.

"Yeah, we're having a few people over."

"You know I have to work tonight."

"That's the whole point, right William?" Libby whispers. William doesn't answer.

"And you know I don't like parties when I'm not here."

"That's not my problem," Graham says.

"Don't speak to me like that!"

Becca leans on Libby, and William sighs, resting his head back on the wall, closing his eyes.

The door slams, and we all jump a little. A few moments pass before the engine of the old station wagon starts up. Libby's mother always revs the engine loudly before switching it into gear. A couple of times William has let Libby and me drive the car down the dirt driveway to the main road, so I can picture Libby's mom sitting on the torn seat, which is covered with one of those beaded things that's incredibly uncomfortable that's supposed to be good for your back. The gearshift is on the steering column and the car kind of jumps forward when you move the lever from neutral to drive. The first time I tried it, I said to William, knowledgeably, "And you're suppose to rev the engine a lot first, right?"

He looked at me for a while and then said, "No, you don't need to do that, that's just Mom's style."

Also her style is somehow managing to spin the tires fast enough so that when she takes off, the pebbles in the driveway splatter against the windows of the living room. At some point, one was big enough that it had cracked the window, which has been that way as long as I've been coming there. I wonder, does she know that she kicks up those stones every time? This time, with us being right next to the window, it sounds like a couple of people firing B.B. guns. Which wouldn't surprise me that much, either.

"Jesus," William murmurs.

"Bitch!" is Graham's final word from the kitchen. A bit late I think, if it was meant for Libby's mom. "I say we call the game over," William says, pushing himself up, not waiting for any of us to agree.

5.

William's footsteps stop, and I hear the dial on the old wall phone rotate slowly back as he quickly dials each number. There were two other phones in the house that I would use first if I were making a call right now.

"Who the hell do you think you're calling?" Graham wants to know.

"Yeah, hello, Dan?" William's voice sounds higher than usual. I've never heard him sound pissed off before, but now I know what he sounds like when he is. "We're not going to have the party over here, so can we come to your house instead? Good, see you around seven."

I hear him throw the heavy receiver up on the wall, stomp out of the kitchen and up the stairs, and slam his bedroom door. His room is really a closet that he's moved into because he can't stand sharing a room with Graham. It isn't bad though and it even has a little window with four panes and a view down to the pond. Libby took me in there once to show me his collection of butterflies that he has in a glass case.

I look at Libby to see what she might be thinking, but she isn't giving me a clue. She's looking back into my eyes, and I think she's just staring, unfocused. But then something changes and I see her watching the way my eyes move, or checking out their color or something. I think it's a cool thing to do, like the staring game I play with my mother's cat, so I look back into her eyes. It's pretty dark behind the couch, but I still see her pupils, light blue with little dark flecks that float around inside the iris.

Becca shifts a little and it makes me look away, and I can't tell if Becca is sleeping or not. She's facing Libby, nestled in under her arm. Even though she hasn't moved for ten minutes, there's something about the way she's holding her back, inflexible like a turtle's shell, that makes me think she's pretending. She isn't breathing in a relaxed, sleepy way either, as though she doesn't want to breathe too loudly because the noise from her breath might drown out essential information. Like I used to do when I was younger, when my parents would argue in the car, at night, coming home from dinner. I would just pretend to go to sleep and they couldn't involve me, ask me questions. I wasn't accountable. It was just easier that way.

"Mommy doesn't want us to have a party because Mommy isn't going to be here, and Mommy's little baby does everything he's supposed to, right?" Graham roared up at William from the bottom of the stairs into the silence. "You are so lame. Fucking Mr. Goody-Two Shoes."

"It ain't that big a deal," says Caleb after Graham bangs the wall hard with his hand. Caleb the diplomat, not a role I ever pictured him in. "Dan's parents are out of town for the whole weekend visiting his sister at school. I know, cuz my mom's supposed to go over there and feed their horses, so it'll be better anyway. Total freedom. We can party till dawn."

"And what about our equipment? How are we supposed to get our speakers and our guitars there? Strap them to my bike?"

I liked the thought of that a lot. Graham, wobbling around off balance on his stupid motorcycle with his gear jerry-rigged on, him having to put his feet down on one side or the other for the mile or so between Libby's house and Dan's house, in and out of potholes in the road, up past the geese at the Peterson's farm that run out nipping at anything that passes by. And by the old graveyard that dates back to the late 1700's where there's a small gravestone made of slate that faces the opposite way from all the others. The story goes, according to Libby's mother, that a girl is buried there who did something awful, though no one knows exactly what it was she did. It has nothing carved on it except the initials D.K. Libby and Becca are in the habit of loudly sucking in their breath and holding it as we pass by the grave. Libby had explained that it was to keep the girl's evil spirit away. I held mine quietly, not actually believing the whole thing, but not really wanting to risk the chance of something happening to me, either. Maybe Graham's guitar would fall off right there and he would have to put it back on, pretending he wasn't in front of the graveyard, like it didn't matter at all. It probably wouldn't do him any good to hold his breath, anyway.

"I'll get my brother to bring the truck over. He'll want to go to the party, too, anyway. Broke up with his girlfriend and I'm sure he'll be looking around for something warm to keep him happy."

"The warmest thing he'll probably find will be some tequila or some Acapulco Gold."

I stick my tongue out at Libby and make a quiet throwing up noise. When I think of Caleb's brother, I think of two things: His habit of always holding his fingers up to his nose, his nostrils flaring as he sniffs them, completely unconcerned if anyone is watching, and once I saw him, in the middle of a conversation with someone, walk fifteen feet away, turn around, and then pee while he was still talking.

"That'll have to do him then," Caleb snorts.

"How are we going to get out of here without them seeing us?" Libby whispers. That's my thought exactly.

"Is Becca really sleeping?" I ask, trying to determine if she is going to rouse herself or if we're going to have to carry her out of here. Becca makes a growling noise like she's just waking up.

"How long did I sleep?" She's speaking in the type of yawn where your mouth is too wide and the yawn is too loud. She's definitely been faking.

"Shhhh!" Libby warns.

I quickly think about the room, where the doors and windows are because I am not interested in Graham suddenly remembering the game and us because there's nothing else to focus his craziness on for a few seconds.

"I could crawl over to the window which is already open a bit, open it wider and then we could all climb through it to the outside. The bulkhead to the basement is on the other side, so it's not too far a drop." My spy training from when I was about ten is always at the ready.

"But I'm really thirsty," Becca whines. She would never be a good spy.

"Too bad," Libby says. "Graham and Caleb are in the kitchen right now." I wonder if Libby doesn't realize that Becca has been faking sleep. "If you're still thirsty when we get outside, you can drink out of the hose." Becca's little mouth is in her usual pout.

"You gotta open the window slowly or else it'll squeak," Libby directs me. I crawl out from behind the couch, feeling safe because Caleb and Graham are still talking and laughing. I stand up and put my palms inside the top of the frame. If I put them underneath the window, I'm afraid that I'll move it up too quickly and it will make a noise like my bedroom window does at home. From the top I have more control to inch it up. The window goes up more easily than I'd thought, without a sound, and there is plenty of room to climb through. I stick my head through it to make sure that the bulkhead is closed, and it is. Someone was actually smart enough to close it when it was raining, which isn't always the case. The someone, I'm sure, is William.

I look at Libby and give her an "all clear" wave. Rather than crawling across the room, she and Becca run over on their feet, their backs stooped. What do you know; they have a little bit of a spy thing going on, too.

"I'll go through first, then Becca, then you, Libby." I can't hear Graham and Caleb talking anymore, and I hope that doesn't mean they're moving around or stopping to think about something else besides their party. I realize I really want to get out of here and I almost don't care if Libby and Becca are caught after I get through. If they are, I might just have to run down the driveway and leave them here. I could keep going until I get home. It won't be getting totally dark for another hour or so, and if it does get dark, it doesn't matter. In fact, it would be nice to walk at night now that the rain has stopped. I could probably see some stars; maybe even find Cassiopeia or the Pleiades. I don't have any shoes on, but my feet are pretty tough after the summer, and anyway, they would just get tougher after the walk, and that's good.

But here's Becca, pushing herself from the windowsill onto the bulkhead without any help, landing on her feet, and Libby is right behind her.

"Quick, let's run over to the barn," Libby says. I am so happy to be back out in the air again. The wind is blowing cool and fresh, whipping leaves around the yard. The sun is in and out of the racing clouds as it starts to set over the ridge of pine trees beyond the hay-field. The grass seems to have grown during the rainstorm and its dampness tickles my feet and makes my ankles itch. We all run over to the barn, to the upper part where the tractor is sometimes put away, and where the bales of hay are stacked high to the ceiling. The barn cat, Harold, greets us by meowing frantically and running straight toward me.

I have a problem with Harold. Cats usually find me wherever I go and they want to be my friend. If I am in a crowd of people, say at a cocktail party with my parents, the cat of the house will not wend its way through the forest of legs to its owner, but to me, and rub its back up against my legs. In most cases, I am happy to at least rub the cat's head, between its ears, often picking it up, as it relaxes, purring, into my arms. The thing is, Harold has weeping eyes filled with yellowish gunk. That says one thing to me: infection.

When I first came over to Libby's house at the beginning of the summer, I saw him and I couldn't believe how awful he looked, a far cry from my mother's fluffy Persian, Millie, that visits the groomer once a month.

"Your cat is sick and you should take him to the vet," I announced, feeling that I had been the first person to observe this, and therefore had the responsibility to alert others as quickly as possible.

Libby's father was there, on a rare visit back from wherever it is he goes. "Just the God damned barn cat," he spat. "If I could see it long enough, I'd shoot it. Never seems to catch any mice judging from the holes in the grain bags." A short time after that I learned that no one fed Harold. "Daddy says that if we feed him, he'll never catch any mice," Becca informed me.

Usually I have some notice before we go to the barn so I can sneak something out of the kitchen, like a little cheese. If I'm really thinking ahead I bring something from my house and keep it in my pocket, then think up some excuse to go out to the barn and feed him. But today, here I am, all upset anyway and to make it worse, Harold is rubbing his bumpy spine and his greasy fur that's coming out in hunks, up and down my leg with what seems like even more vigor than usual. I watch him, helpless. "Later, Harold," I say.

There is no way I can pet him, so I pull my sleeve over my hand and pat him on his head with my covered forearm. I'm glad it's Libby's shirt, not mine. It seems to help a little because he's stopped his pathetic yowling, though not his intense rubbing.

Libby is at the side of the barn turning on the squeaky faucet to the hose. The water trickles out and Becca starts walking towards it.

"Wait," Libby says. "Let me check the temperature of the water before you drink it." She walks over and picks up the hose and holds her hand under the stream. "It's fine," she says, handing it over to Becca, pointing it away so that she can't get wet. Sometimes, if the hose is out in the sun all day, the water is hot, but it's been quite cool and raining, so I think she did it out of habit, not thinking. Becca holds the hose in one hand and drinks and drinks out of the stream, like a thirsty puppy. As I watch her I notice that she looks red in her cheeks. I think maybe it's because we've been running, but we haven't run that far. Libby notices too, because she leans over and takes the hose away from her sister and drops it onto the ground so that the water goes into the grass. She places the palm of her hand on Becca's forehead and slides it down inside the back of her shirt.

"You're freezing!" says Becca squirming so that Libby is forced to take her hand away.

"And you're boiling. Open your mouth." Becca does as she's told, tilts her head back, and sticks her tongue out. It is a ritual that I've seen all summer. "Probably strep again," Libby says, sounding pleased with her diagnosis. She cradles Becca's chin in between her thumb and her forefinger and peers inside her mouth. "Of course, I can't see anything without my flashlight, but I bet that's it." Becca seems to get strep as often as most people get a sniffle.

I walk back over to the barn to turn the faucet off because I can't stand to see the water pouring into the grass, being wasted.

"We better take her into the house and give her some antibiotic," Libby says. All this sneaking around and now we're going to walk right back in there in front of them. Great! In the distance I hear the low roar of an engine slowly coming down the drive and a barking dog.

"Definitely the yellow truck," I say, knowing that everyone calls it "Yellowtruck" like one word, but I don't want to be that familiar with it.

"I'll be glad to see it for once," Libby says. "Let's wait here for a minute." We can't sit on the grass because it's still damp, so we just stand there and wait as it gets closer. I can't see the front porch, but the screen door keeps slamming, so I assume that Graham and Caleb are walking in and out with their equipment. Libby looks over towards the house.

"They'll be gone soon," I say.

Yellowtruck appears through the trees, bucking its way slowly over the bumps. In the back, trying to keep his balance is Caleb's dog, a shepherdy mutt who accompanies the family everywhere, barking constantly. We just stand there, aware that we are just standing there, not even caring to pretend that we are doing something else. Caleb's older brother and some other guy that I don't remember ever seeing before, though who knows because most of those guys look the same to me, are in the cab. Reggie—I finally remember that's Caleb's brother's name—is leaning over the steering wheel, both hands and forearms resting on the top of it like he is relaxing in a slow dance—not likely—or more like just propping himself up. His friend is pounding on the dashboard as if he's playing the bongos, though as far as I can hear, they haven't fixed the radio, and the coat hanger that used to sit in the antenna hole is gone.

The driveway ends where Libby's mother always parks the car, but they keep driving the truck right onto the lawn and we slowly walk after it so we can see how close they'll take it to the house. They take it up alongside the porch, but it doesn't quite suit them so they pull the truck up and back a few times so that the back of the bed is just even with the porch floor. They make deep tire tracks in the lawn so we can see inches of dirt underneath. Finally, they turn off the truck, which shudders for a few seconds before resting. The dog keeps on barking, always in the same position, its head pointing up at the sky, yap yap, yap yap yap, at nothing, like it likes hearing itself bark. Reggie and his friend just sit there, occasionally looking over at us and laughing, occasionally looking down at their laps.

I look at Libby; she is standing behind Becca mouthing, "rolling a joint." I nod thinking, already completely stoned. Graham and Caleb are distracted enough that I move forward to get a better look. Libby and Becca follow behind me.

Graham walks out onto the porch and lifts up one of the amps that's sitting there by a strap that's attached to the top of it. It must be very heavy, because his arm muscles are tight and he has to rest the amp on his leg for support as he walks with it, kind of kicking it with his shin to keep it up. He steps onto the truck and it bounces a bit under his weight. He walks with it all the way back to the cab, through the barking and the beer cans that are rolling around. He leans down and pounds his fist on the back window.

"Earth to Yellowtruck," he shouts. "Do you think you guys are capable of helping us with this equipment?" The rusty passenger door squeaks open and both Reggie and his friend slide out.

"Still haven't figured out how to fix the other door?" Graham says to Caleb, turning his back on the stoners who are already bent over double giggling uncontrollably about something that is very amusing, to them.

"I'm glad Reggie isn't trying to climb out of the driver's window like he usually does," Libby says.

Graham and Caleb are in more of a rhythm now loading all their stuff. The other two have gone to sit at the far end of the porch, which is still puddled up in places, to have a smoke.

"That's it," Graham says, slamming up the tailgate, which doesn't catch right away, so he has to unlatch it and push it hard a few more times.

"You girls coming with us to the party?" Caleb shouts. Graham's standing next to him, his arms folded across his chest. He mutters something to Caleb that we can't hear, but Caleb smiles, lifting his armpit up and scratching it, slowly, playing with his hair that's caked with a white streak of antiperspirant.

Libby's ready. "Becca's got a fever and I think she's got strep again." She knows her brother and there's one thing he doesn't like: people being sick. He regards it as a weakness, and he especially can't stand it when Becca's sick.

"What about you," Caleb says, pointing the finger at me that's just been twirling his armpit hairs. "You ain't sick."

"I'm staying here with Libby," I say, my voice cracking.

Graham's staring at all of us and I prepare for what's coming, but all he shouts is, "You're all fucking babies." He jumps off the porch and faces the house and looks up at the window where William's room is. "Did you hear me?" he shouts for William. "You're all fucking babies." There's no response from the other side of the little panes.

"Let's go," Graham says, holding onto the top of the cab and lowering himself through the window into the driver's seat. Caleb walks around to the passenger's side and opens the door as the waste-cases climb in. Graham starts up the engine and drives right at us, like he's going to run us over, Caleb struggling to pull the heavy door shut. Libby holds her ground and so does Becca, and he veers away before he gets too close. I stare at him and think to myself, what a jerk, what a jerk, what a jerk. But I don't let my mouth form the words, it's only in my brain because I'm not brave enough to really let him know what I'm thinking. He and I lock eyes for a moment and he gives me that sweet look again, but just as he does he honks the horn and makes us all jump, laughing triumphantly. We watch as they disappear down the driveway, the four of them crammed in the cab with the barking dog, and the equipment in the back.

"Good riddance," I say, something my mother always says. As I walk towards the house with the girls, I find myself spreading my arms straight out, circling them up and down. It's incredibly quiet with the only sounds the wind rustling the leaves and a single crow cawing. The only person left, other than us is William, and I hope it will stay that way for a while.

6

Becca and I follow Libby into the kitchen where she heads directly to the refrigerator. She opens it up and reaches up to the top shelf where the bottle of pink medicine is. It's half-full and looks like oil and vinegar dressing before you shake it. The bottom of the liquid is thick and dark pink and the top is almost translucent.

"Sit down at the table," Libby says as she reaches in the drawer for a clean spoon. There isn't one, so she reaches into the sink and takes one out of the standing dishwater and rinses it off. She pours the liquid into the spoon and tips it into Becca's mouth, Becca looking like a baby bird in a nest. Libby places the bottle down on the table and I pick it up. The label says it expired six months ago, and it also says "use until finished."

"Libby, did you notice this stuff expired a while ago?" I say nicely, matter-of-factly, not to diminish her attempts at nursing.

"Mom says it never expires, that it's just a way for the American Medical Association to keep doctors in business. You have to pay a doctor to tell you that you need it, and then you have to buy the stuff. It's a total rip-off." It sounds like Libby's mother talking, not her, so it isn't worth mentioning that you are supposed to use the whole bottle.

"And Mom says you don't need anywhere near the dosage it says on the bottle, that's just so you'll use more too," she says, reading my thoughts. My parents are skeptical about some aspects of modern medicine too, like they didn't believe in giving me all the required immunizations when I was a baby. But this is different. Becca is still sick. That is, if she really is sick. Sometimes I'm not sure if they aren't playing some kind of advanced game of hospital.

I hear measured walking down the stairs and William appears in the doorway. He doesn't look angry like I thought he might.

"Becca sick again?" he asks. Libby nods. "Mind if I go for a bike ride, or is she really sick?" Even though we love William, the thought of being by ourselves in the house makes us quite relieved and a little excited. We shake our heads "no."

"You going to the party?" Libby asks.

"Probably not." William walks over to Becca and kisses her on the top of her head like she is a little kitten and she smiles, pushing her head gently towards him for another one. He gives it to her, waves to us, and disappears out the door.

"Well, we can do anything we want now, anything at all," Libby says. She doesn't sound that excited about it, like she's just trying to sound happy; and I don't feel excited about it either. I actually feel really lonely, but I don't know why. The house that usually seems too small and cramped and tense, seems huge and empty.

"We can watch any show we want," Becca says. This is her idea of freedom. Not mine. Libby looks at Becca.

"I think you should probably go up to bed and rest," she says.

"But I don't want to go up there by myself," she whines. "It's too spooky."

Libby sighs. We aren't free at all.

"O.K.," Libby says. "You go upstairs, quickly get your pajamas on and then you can come downstairs and I'll set up the couch so it's really cozy for you, and you can watch whichever show you want."

At first I think, what about us? And then I realize that Libby's concocting a way in which Becca will be distracted so that we can do something else.

Becca thinks this is a fine idea and no longer listless, she runs up the stairs. Libby opens the fridge and puts the medicine away, reaches down into the shelves on the inside of the door and pulls out two dark green beer bottles by their necks. "After she's settled in," she smiles, holding them up like prizes.

Now this is a little freedom. My father has been letting me sip beer out of his mug since I was a baby, but to actually possess and hold an entire beer is not something I've been privileged to do. Libby quietly slides the bottles back into place among the others and shuts the door.

We walk into the living room, renewed by our secret, and Libby pushes the television around so that it faces the couch.

I take the blankets that are crumpled up in the corner of the couch and shake them out, dust and lint flying everywhere. I spread one out on the bottom of the couch and the other on the top. I smooth them out and take all the pillows that are scattered about and place them where Becca's head will be. Then, I turn the top of the blanket back, like how they always do to my bed when I stay in hotels. I turn on the light, which sits on the table next to the couch. Then I walk into the kitchen, get a plate, put some cookies on it, and pour Becca a glass of cranberry juice, her favorite. I think it will be good for her throat. It's the gross kind though, and it actually says on the label that it's made with only two percent juice.

I take the food back into the living room and place it on the table with the lamp.

"There," I announce.

"Whoa," she says. It's her favorite expression for when she's really pleased. "Where did you learn to do that?" I stop smiling. I think of Graham sliding into the truck through the window, his hands holding the roof of the truck, the same hands that had held mine. I look back at her and make myself smile.

Becca appears around the corner with her pajamas and even a robe on. She takes one look and smiles like I haven't seen her smile before. She runs across the floor, scuffing her slippers in a happy dance and makes a leap onto her new bed. She slides carefully underneath the covers, trying not to unsmooth them, keeping them tight. I guess I made the couch-bed for her because she really doesn't have her own bed. She either sleeps with Libby or sometimes Libby's mother, or sometimes in a sleeping bag on Libby's floor. She reaches over and takes a sip of the juice and smiles a big red dye smile.

Becca has no idea what's happening to her. I feel kind of bad we're doing all these nice things for her for selfish reasons, but I don't care so much that it stops me. Even though I'm not sure what we're going to do when we get her settled in. But I think it's fun just to see if we can distract her enough by totally spoiling her. Which, of course, we can.

Mary Martin's *Peter Pan* is just beginning, a special, and Libby goes over and feels her head again.

"You still feel pretty warm, maybe you need some Tylenol." Libby walks out and brings back a large white bottle that has "extra strength" in big blue letters at the top. Knowing that only two years or so ago, after a discussion with my pediatrician, my parents had decided that I was ready to go from the bubble gum flavored children's ones to the adult ones, I speak up. "That stuff might be a little strong for her."

"Cynthia, you're always so afraid of everything. Lighten up," says my friend. It is true, or seems to be true now, that I am more cautious than Libby, but this time I have some facts to hold on to.

"When I was sick, my pediatrician told my parents in front of me that it's best to take the children's kind until you're seventy pounds or so, and then you're only supposed to take one of the regular kind, not the extra strength ones."

"Well, she's had this kind before and she has a fever. What do you want to have happen, her have a seizure because her temperature spikes up?" Libby snaps open the bottle cap and shakes four tablets out into her hand. She goes over to the juice that I've so carefully poured and offers them to Becca.

"You know I can't swallow pills," Becca, the invalid, reminds her.

Libby puts down the juice, avoids me looking at her and goes back into the kitchen. I hear pounding and presume that she's pulverizing the Tylenol.

"Here you go," says Libby, confidently, reassuringly, as she sweeps by me. Clearly, there's nothing for me to say. Besides, I'm not completely sure that she's totally wrong. I don't think that there's a potential for major overdose, I just don't think it's the best solution. Like maybe one is just fine.

"I'm going to miss my favorite part," Becca moans, turning her head away.

"I crushed them and put them in your favorite cherry yogurt," Libby says, offering her a large pink and white spoonful while clicking the television to pause with her other hand. Becca opens wide and the delivery's made.

"Yuck," Becca pouts. "I can taste the medicine."

Libby immediately sticks the spoon inside the container and scoops the jammy part out of the bottom and mixes in just a little plain yogurt. Becca's waiting.

"More," she chirps. Libby spoon-feeds her the rest and Becca leans back in her bed. "You can start it now," she says. Libby reaches over and turns off the light, and I realize that it's become pretty dark outside. "See, it's like your own movie theater."

Libby gets up, mission accomplished. "Cynthia, can you help do the dishes for a minute?"

I follow her into the kitchen, knowing why she's suddenly become chore-conscious. "Look," she whispers, "I'll open the beer and as we do the dishes we can reach into the refrigerator and take sips. So in case anyone comes, or Becca suddenly shows up, we can put the bottles right back in."

She opens the refrigerator and quickly twists the caps off, leaving them balanced on the top of each bottle.

I look into the dishwater that is brown and has rice and pasta and some kind of spinach thing floating on the top of it. "You got any rubber gloves?" I ask.

"Maybe under the sink." I open the doors and find two gloves stuck together sitting in a pot with a broken handle. I pull them apart and they are both right hands, stained with something brown. I put them on, even though the left one is backwards, because there's no way I'm going to stick my hands into the bilge, unprotected.

I plunge my hands in and pick up a dish and start to scrub it with a dish brush that has white goo trapped in its short plastic bristles. This is ridiculous, washing the dishes with stagnant water. I resubmerge the dish and reach down, searching for the plug. I yank on it. There are a couple of bubbles and then nothing happens.

"Does this sink drain, or what?" I ask. Libby is right there with my beer. "I don't even want to touch the bottle with my gloves," I say. Libby the provider giggles and comes after my lips with the open bottle. Helpless, I can't do anything but drink as she slowly tips back the steamy cold bubbles into my throat. I try to keep up with her tipping, but after about five little gulps, there is no way I can. I let out a muffled noise as a warning and then pull away. She tips a little longer and some of the beer splashes on the floor, some of it on my shirt, actually her shirt.

"Nice one," I say as she grabs the wet rag that has been sitting next to the faucet. She throws it onto the wood floor and smooshes it around with her foot, making even more of a mess. She's laughing, and I look at her and the dishes and dirty water everywhere, and I think it's pathetic, but somehow it seems funny and I start to laugh too.

"Libby," Becca wails. We stop laughing and Libby quickly puts the bottles back into their safety spot.

"Coming," she calls. There's a half a package of Lifesavers on the windowsill above the sink and Libby pops two into her mouth as she heads out of the room. I look back at the dishwater, problem still unsolved. Whatever. I'll just wash them in the other sink with running water. I push the faucet arm over and turn on the hot water, which comes out in something just slightly more powerful than a trickle, which I understand means the well is low, even after the rain. I place a dish underneath it and decide to abandon the plastic brush, thinking that my finger covered with the glove will do just as good a job at scraping.

"She wants some more juice, but it looks like she's going to nod off any minute," Libby says opening the refrigerator. As she goes in for the cranberry drink, she takes a quick swig of her beer. Back out she goes with Becca's drink.

I'm feeling pretty weird, nothing feels right. My best friend, who I think I know, is acting strange. Even before she drank the beer. In fact, the whole family is acting even stranger than usual. But maybe it's me. Maybe I'm the one who's seeing everything differently and everything is the same. That's it, there's something weird with me.

But what about Graham? Is he acting weird or what? Is he thinking he wants to be my boyfriend?

The dishes don't really seem clean to me, even though there is no more obvious crud hiding in the brown flower pattern of the plates or in the bottoms of the coffee mugs.

"She's asleep!" Libby whispers as she runs back through and hugs me.

"Great!" I say, trying to feel like her, share her new energy. I've had enough of this chilly dishwater mood. I can't quite get there, though. I can't see what is really great, but I do want to have fun. Libby opens the refrigerator and grabs both bottles. She hands me one and starts gulping out of the other.

"Didn't you get them mixed up?" I say, noting that mine is half full and I can only remember having taken five little sips, while the one she's chugging down is just about full.

"Afraid of getting my germs?" she says, lowering her beer, putting her face inches away from mine. I bring the bottle to my lips and stick my tongue into the opening so only a little beer flows through into my mouth. I'm not sure that I even like the way it tastes.

"So I wonder if Graham left any pot here," she says, finishing off the bottom of the bottle. She carefully balances it in a paper bag on the kitchen floor that is about to fall over, overflowing with other returnables. She's incredibly casual.

"What if he did?" I ask.

"I don't know, I thought it might be fun to try some."

"Yeah, right. I can't wait to inhale smoke into my lungs and then act like Reggie and his stupid friend." I pick up a fork that I've just cleaned and hold it in front of me. "Wow, this is amazing. Hey man, have you ever really looked at a fork before? Have you ever counted how many tines a fork has? I mean this one has four, but do they all have four? I mean, who thought up the idea for a fork, why do we even use forks? Wow!" I throw myself into a kitchen chair, like I'm totally exhausted, like looking at the fork has completely tired me out. Libby's laughing hard, so I keep doing things I've seen the boys do, exaggerated. I pretend to nod out, then sit up just before my head hits the table, saying, "Man, this is good weed." I scratch my face and stare at nothing, then get up, open the cookie tin and stuff graham crackers in my face.

"Munchies, man," I say. I get it so right that neither of us can believe it and we both laugh really hard together, so much that we're on the floor with tears streaming down both our faces, the salt adding a delicious taste to the sweetness in my mouth. I love to make Libby laugh.

I'm feeling better now and Libby says, "Let's go outside." It sounds good. "I'll be back in a minute," she says as she goes toward the living room. I pull on my sweater I'd taken off earlier in the day when it was raining, another long time ago.

7

"It's a star."

"No, it isn't. It's a satellite. It's moving," Libby says as she slides deeper into her sleeping bag so that just her head's visible. She keeps squinting her eyes, then opening them wide. It can't be helping her to see. Anyway she's never had problems seeing things from a distance before.

"The clouds are moving. Look again," I say, pointing my little flashlight into space. There's movement from inside the sleeping bag and her hand appears holding a bottle. She doesn't sit up to drink it, she just tips it back a bit, her neck stiffening as she tries to ensure it goes in her mouth and not all over her face and the sleeping bag. I look into the eastern sky. East is where my parents are. It's cool to think that my dad can look up at the sky where he is and he might be able to see some of the same constellations that I can, the ones he taught me.

"Test time," I say, shining the light on her. Sometimes we play the name-the-constellations-game.

"The Little Dipper," an easy first question.

"I don't want to play." She takes another sip and reaches out of the bag, rolling over to the side with her long elbowy arm and awkwardly twists the bottle into a patch of dirt just beyond the tarp we're squeezed on top of. I shine the flashlight on the bottle and through the dark glass I can see that there's just a little beer left. A darker line rings the bottom.

Maybe it's too boring a start, so I choose her favorite, to get her going. "Find Cassiopeia then." It used to be my favorite, before I decided I liked the Pleiades better. I decided I didn't want her favorite to be my favorite; besides, it's been my favorite for a long time. So when she told me it was her favorite, I thought maybe I should think of something new.

She smiles, she knows what I'm doing and she likes it. I'm treating her like she treats Becca, getting her to do something that she doesn't want to do by showing her that I know her, by showing her how close we are.

"No." She shakes her head with big shakes.

"Are you drunk or something?" I inquire.

"I don't think a person can get drunk on three beers," she slurs. I count four. Two inside and two outside.

"I don't suppose you can walk a straight line," I offer, thinking of a drunkenness indicator. Without answering Libby pushes herself out of her sleeping bag and stands in her turtleneck and underpants, her hands on her hips. "Okay, where's the line?" she demands. I look around quickly with my flashlight and see a large stick that will do well to make a mark in the ground. I pull myself out of my warm cocoon into the damp night air and grab the stick. The spot we are encamped on is a bit of rock that sticks out of the hayfield. There's dirt and moss that covers the rock quite a bit, so it's a soft place to sleep and we tend to not get as dewy here as when we sleep in the tall grass of the field. Besides, from here we feel far enough away from the house, but we can still see the silhouette of Becca's body against the back of the couch, the blueness of the television lighting the room, her tape having ended hours ago.

I firmly dig the stick into the ground and pull it slowly along, making as deep a hole as I can. The line itself isn't totally straight, because I keep hitting stones that are just below the surface, but it's good enough. It's about twelve feet long, long enough for a fair test. "There you go," I point with my stick, in full schoolmistress mode. She walks, very seriously, over to the line.

"Should I just walk any way I want?"

"Like medium steps in 'Mother May I'." That gives her more information than she can handle. She can't remember what medium steps are, of course, so she does baby steps, the kind where you walk heel to toe, heel to toe.

"Rrrrrrr." I make the sound of a disqualification buzzer and she falls to the ground and rocks back and forth in a little ball, laughing out of control. Her laugh doesn't sound like the laugh she usually has, it sounds shallow and forced, like she's listening to the sound of it. After a minute or two any humor that's possibly in the situation has definitely come and gone, but Libby's still enjoying hugging herself and rocking, though she isn't laughing any more.

"Enough!" I say, holding out my hand for her. She keeps rocking. "Come on." I don't like this scene at all.

"Libby, you're going to freeze," is all I can think of. So, of course, the thing that makes no sense stops her. She sits up and crosses her legs and looks right at me. Her eyes look huge. "Was that some weird yoga move?" I say, trying to make her laugh. She suddenly leans forward and wraps her arms around my neck so that her forehead bangs into mine.

"I love you," she mumbles. Oh my God, I think. She must be really drunk. And with that, she starts crying. Sobbing, actually.

"What's the matter?" I ask, pushing her hair back from her face. She won't look up and her tears are so big they're leaving huge stains on her turtleneck. Now what am I supposed to do? She's crying so hard that she's sucking in her breath and shaking.

"Libby," I say firmly, holding her shoulders in my hands. It's pretty cold and a little breeze occasionally blows across us, making the night chillier. Once, I saw a friend of William's and his girlfriend take their separate sleeping bags, unzip them all the way and then zip them up together to make one huge bag. I hadn't watched exactly how they'd done it, but I liked it. She's shaking like crazy, though, and maybe we ought to go inside where it'll be warmer, where there are blankets and I can give her some chamomile tea or something. But first I'll try to solve things out here.

I unzip my bag all the way around so that it's completely open. I try Libby's zipper, but it gets stuck at the bottom on the first curve. I struggle with it, trying to figure out if it's caught on something, and it won't move. I step back and knock over the bottle she'd ground into the earth.

"Get back in your sleeping bag," I order. She crawls back in and I take my sleeping bag and place the bottom of it under her and the top of it over her like a giant envelope with me inside. She's shaking so violently that I think this might be what people refer to when they use the word "convulsions," but I'm not sure. I pull the sleeping bags over our heads and take her hands, her freezing ice blocks, in my hands and put them to my mouth to blow hot air on them.

"I think we'd better go inside," I say. "It's late and it would be better if we're in there with Becca anyway."

"I can't move," she chatters. Don't be stupid, you just moved, I think, but instead I say, "I'll help you." I open up my bag and stand up. "Can you try to walk down to the house?"

"I think I'm going to throw up," she moans. She crawls out of the sleeping bag, off the tarp and starts heading toward the field. I know that when I had the flu last winter I didn't want anyone near me while I threw up, but the next moment I wanted lots of sympathy, so I don't know if I ought to follow her or not. Suddenly, I hear a branch snap behind the rotting oak tree that is on the border between the field and the knolly part where we're set up. There are a lot of brambles there and an old barbwire fence that is waist high in places, ground level in others.

"I don't care if you throw up in front of me," I say. "Besides, remember the fence?"

A second snap, somehow longer, like something heavy pressing down on it and breaking it slowly, comes from the same place as the first. The first one could have just been a random outside noise, like a squirrel, which we've woken up, because we're making so much noise. If it was further away, it might be a deer. They always browse around at night, but they're too skittish to be so close to us, so that idea makes no sense. I feel the cold and something else. I'm scared.

I quickly follow her, like you follow a baby who's headed directly for a wood stove, not caring if she barfs all over me. I put my arm underneath her arm, her arm over my shoulder, like I've seen in war photographs in Life magazine, and swing her up onto her feet. She manages to turn her face away from me before throwing up, and then throwing up again.

"I'm so sorry Cynthia," she cries.

"It's okay," I say. What else am I supposed to say? I don't want to make things worse.

"No I mean it. I'm really, really sorry." As she speaks, she shakes her head and little bits of vomit clinging to her face fly off onto my shirt. Really nice going, Libby.

"Down to the house," I say. "We'll get you out of these clothes and get you into something warmer. How about taking a bath?"

"I'm so sorry," she groans before puking all over my arm. The juice moves like lava down to my hand that's holding her up. The warmth of it on my skin and the smell make me gag, but someone has to keep things together, so I take a deep breath of the night air, look at the stars and help her drag her stumbling body toward the house. How much food can she have in her stomach to throw up? The bile has to be nearing the end. I'm trying to remember what I've seen her eat today. Oh yeah, oatmeal cookies for breakfast.

As we get closer to the house, away from the uneasiness of the night, I can see through the window that Becca is still in her same position, sleeping, thank goodness. No need for her to see this.

"Up the steps," I say, reminding Libby that they're there and that it would be helpful if she could try to place her feet on them for me. She wavers about a bit, but she puts her feet where they're supposed to go. She leans forward a little and gags a bit, but nothing comes out. Maybe we're past the worst of it.

"Is Becca okay?" Libby shouts as we pass through the door, after I very carefully hold onto her while I ease the screen door shut with one hand, so that Becca won't hear it and wake up.

"Shhhhhhh!" I warn. "She's fine. She's still sleeping."

"But I really need to tell her I love her," she whispers loudly.

"Not now!"

"Are you telling me that I can't tell my little sister I love her?" I have to rescue the situation fast. "Your shirt is really smelly," I say. "If Becca smells it she'll be upset and remember, she isn't feeling well, so why don't you just get cleaned up a little and then we'll come back down and then you can tell her." I grab her hand and head toward the stairs like there's no option. Luckily, she decides to follow. "Hold onto the railing," I demand.

Up we go. I push open the door to her room and she walks in and throws herself on her back onto the bed. Her face and shirt and legs have vomit on them so I go to get a washcloth in the bathroom. There's one still folded, sitting on the sink, so I put just the corner of it under the faucet, rinsing my vomitty arm and hand under the water as well and bring it back into her. There she is, her mouth open in a deep snore.

I don't want to wake her up, but I also can't let her spend the night sleeping covered in that mess. In a way, it would serve her right to be reminded of what she's done, but it's just too gross. I can actually see oatmeal flakes and raisins in the sticky little globs. I lift up her limp arm and push one of the messes into the washcloth. I realize that I'm going to need more than one cloth for the job, so I think I better go downstairs and see if there are some paper towels in the kitchen. I sneak back down the stairs, glance through the door at sleeping Becca, and head into the kitchen. Luckily, and remarkably, there is almost a full roll sitting on the counter. I take it off its holder and start to run for the stairs, but at the bottom of the stairs I think I smell pot. I think I must just be mistaking it for something else, and I'm feeling pretty tired myself, so up I go, not wanting to try to figure out what it is. Libby is in the exact same position that I left her in.

I grab her wastebasket and begin to wipe the stuff, bit by bit, off her skin. The paper towels mount up quickly. Her arms are easy, but her legs are covered from her thighs to her ankles. The mess is not as thick there, but it's dried faster and I'm afraid I'll wake her if I scrub too hard. I'm making little red marks on her skin but she doesn't seem fazed, she doesn't move.

I don't know if I should take her shirt off, even though it is completely covered in throw up and wetness, and somehow, even dirt. I feel uncomfortable about it, so I rip off a few pieces of paper towel and blot them on the larger spots so it won't be quite as gross, especially if she rolls over or something.

What is it I remember about Jimi Hendrix? Didn't he throw up in his sleep after a drug overdose and die? Wasn't he supposed to have been drinking too? Or was that Janis Joplin? Or Mama Cass? Or all of them? The point is, there is someone who had either done drugs or drank too much and then they threw up in the middle of the night in their sleep, and because they were lying on their back, they choked and died. This is not going to happen to Libby. If I roll her on her side and put pillows behind her back to keep her there so she can't roll back over, she'll be fine. I do it easily. I just push the pillows behind her and she doesn't miss a breath. I take the comforter that's at the foot of the bed and pull it over her. I sigh so loudly that I surprise myself.

I think it's fine to leave Becca downstairs. Though maybe I should go down one more time to check on her, maybe feel her forehead to see if she's warm because Libby can't, but she looked fine and peaceful just moments ago and I'm feeling exhausted now. I just really want to go to sleep. Great. My sleeping bag is still outside. There's no way I'm going back out there alone. My mother always says to me when I give details of a story, "You're always exaggerating things." So maybe I'm exaggerating what I heard and felt outside, but still, I'm not going out there. I look around the room for what I can sleep on. There's a foam bedroll and Becca's ballerina sleeping bag. They'll do just fine.

I unroll the bedroll and throw the pink sleeping bag on top of it.

I wonder where the perfect spot for me to lay is. It's probably a good idea if I lie on the floor near her, because if, despite my efforts, she does start to choke in her sleep, I'll hear her and stop her. However, I don't want to be right under her because she might step on me in the middle of the night or throw up again. And I don't want to sleep next to her because she still reeks. I decide to lie on the floor at the foot of the bed. The light is still on in the bathroom, which is good, because if Libby does decide to get up, she can find her way easily to the toilet, and if Becca wakes up and is afraid, the bathroom light will light her way up to us. I walk over and push the door so that it's about six inches from being shut so that light will come in just right. I'm so tired that I feel like I'm floating. My body seems far away from my head. I drag the sleeping things next to Libby's bed, and with all my clothes on, I collapse onto the floor.

8.

I'm half asleep, I think, when I smell something different in the room. The smell is not a bad smell, specifically unfamiliar, generally human. I think that Libby must be getting up, so I listen quietly and watch the door through slits in my eyes, because I don't want her to know that I'm awake. It's better if she does what she needs to do, throws up or goes to the bathroom, or whatever, without my assistance. I do not want to take care of her anymore tonight unless it's absolutely necessary. A hand very gently touches my shoulder.

At my side, squatting on his feet, in a tee shirt and very white underwear, is Graham. I'm trying to figure out what's going on, this underwear advertisement looming in front of me. He slides his hand down my arm and fits his fingers in between mine. As he stands up, he pulls me up with him. Libby's in her bed, still propped up, in-case-of-emergency position, and now next to her is Becca. I hadn't heard a thing. How long have I been sleeping?

He leads me out into the little hallway that runs to the back of the house, past William's room, past the closet, past the sewing room to his room, a room that I've only been in once, secretly with Libby. And now I'm being led by him, inside. There's a mattress on the floor and a candle that's sputtering, and a stick of incense burned half way down, smoke rising, ashes fallen on the table.

He sits down on the mattress and he pulls me down with him. I think maybe he's upset or something, because when I look at his face, it seems paler than usual. I think he is going to lecture me about the beer or Libby, but I really don't get it. His eyes are big and watery in the candlelight. He lets go of my hand and reaches behind him and grabs an ashtray that has half a joint in it. He sticks it in his mouth and reaches back again for the matches, strikes one, puts it to the tip and sucks in his breath. I've never sat so close to anyone smoking pot

56

before. I watch him as he sucks in another little breath. "Want some?"

I shake my head. He blows out all the smoke from his lungs and I quietly hold my breath. I can't stand smoke of any kind. He smiles at me and shrugs and takes another hit. Before I know it, he leans over and holds my shoulders, tight, and puts his lips up against mine. He forces his tongue in between my teeth and exhales all his smoke inside me. I struggle against him and he responds by gently pushing me back onto his mattress and lies on top of me, his mouth still locking on mine. I cough, so he pulls his mouth away and cups his hand over my mouth. "Shhhhhh," he whispers sweetly. He stretches over and blows out the candle in one short puff.

He seems very heavy on top of me. At the end of the summer we'd played tag or fooled around with lacrosse sticks where we'd fall against each other. But that's always just for a second or two. The weight of his pelvis seems immense to me and as I think this, he seems to read my mind, gently rocking into me, makes me feel it even more. He keeps one hand on my mouth and slides his hand and arm in between our bodies, down between his legs. There's such a jumble of weight and pressure and movement on top of me in the dark, I can't tell what's going on, except that he's trying to pull down my pants and his at the same time. I'm trapped underneath rhythmic energy that no longer seems like Graham, like a person even. I lie there, first hoping it will end soon, and then relax, resigned, then not thinking at all. My brain has floated so far from my body that I am looking down at myself, from above. The person that can't move is and isn't me.

Now, it stops. He pulls his hand and arm out from between us, from between my legs. He relaxes his other hand that's been holding my mouth, as his whole body exhales on top of me. He lets his arms go limp at our sides and he isn't moving. It feels like I have bricks on my chest. Suddenly, he pushes himself up, leans over, and grabs a pair of pants off the floor. In one motion, he stands up and adjusts himself and pulls them on. He leans over and grabs my hand, pulling me up off the mattress.

"You better go and wash your jeans and shirt, and I guess your skin off," he whispers matter-of-factly. I look down to see what he's talking about and I'm confused. I know I'm supposed to know exactly what's happened, but I don't. And, I don't want him to know that I don't know, so I just nod my head. "Just go in the bathroom and wash yourself and be quiet," he smiles. "Sleep well."

As I start to head toward the door he follows me and takes up my hand so gently and slides my fingers again in between his fingers. He squeezes them slightly, quickly. He takes his thumb and rubs it quickly on the palm of my hand. He looks like he's going to say something else, but he doesn't and then he lets go. I walk back down the dark hallway to the pale light of the little bathroom. I slowly close the door and examine the wetness that seems to have soaked into my clothes already. I do as I'm instructed and pull off the hand towel that's hanging askew from the towel bar. I blot myself, just the way I did to Libby earlier. I keep up the blotting, though it makes no sense, but what does make sense? Nothing at the moment.

The door swings open and I jump. Libby's there, her long hair stuck together like wet hay, her mouth open, and her lips big and dry. She's changed her shirt and her underpants, so at least there appears to be some promise that she might be returning to her usual self.

"I'm so thirsty," she says, her tongue licking her lips trying to get some moisture in them. I don't want to put the towel back on the rack because it's gross, and there's no laundry hamper, so I throw it in the tub on top of my still wet clothes that I threw there yesterday. I can't believe it was only yesterday.

She sits on the toilet and pees immediately, obviously without a thought that I'm standing there. That isn't so unusual, but it usually takes her a while to go. For her, all barriers have been lowered between us, but for me the barriers seem to have shot up. She has no secrets. Suddenly, I have too many.

"How come you're dressed and you're up?" she asks, recognizing that there's something else going on besides her feeling gross. Right now I think I can tell her any story I want, because she's sitting way forward on the toilet looking like she might rest her head on her knees and fall asleep any second, like she's not paying all that much attention.

"I was cold because our sleeping bags are still outside."

"I feel dizzy, Cynthia. If I start thinking about being outside or the sleeping bags or anything, it seems like I'll throw up."

"Then don't think about it. Let's go back to bed." I take a quick glance at my pants and follow her out of the bathroom into the bedroom. I want to look down the hall, but I don't because I know that even the slightest hint might give her an idea, even in her state, that something's happened. I push the door nearly shut. I don't want to close it all the way, so there'll be a small stream of light to see by. I look over at the bed, and see Becca curled up in the middle of it.

"Why don't you sleep on one side of her and I'll sleep on the other," I say, not wanting to go back down on the floor.

"Good thinking," Libby mumbles. She's restraining her mouth in such a way that she won't feel like throwing up. We climb onto the bed and we both grab separate corners of the comforter and pull it up over the three of us. Safe, I think to myself. I go right back to sleep, and I have a falling dream. That's what my dad calls it, where you wake up at the end of a fall because your whole body jolts. You don't really remember the fall because of the shock of the violent waking up part. I wonder if the girls felt my spasm, but I listen and they're both breathing, steadily and quietly. What's different is that the door is open about six inches more than I'd left it. Sometimes there's a draft in the house, but not that much of one. I move closer to Becca. I can feel the heat coming off her. It seems more like soft heat from the coziness of the comforter rather than the bright heat that comes from a fever. I give her the smallest kiss on the back of her shoulder, wishing there was someone here to do the same for me.

When I wake up I know there is no one else in the room. I pull my cheek, wet with drool, off the pillow and roll over just to make sure that the emptiness I feel is real. The other side of the comforter is pushed to the foot of the bed, abandoned for breakfast. I roll back and watch as the breeze blows warmish air into the room, muggy, making the cotton curtain move. I pull my knees up close to my chest and wonder whether I ought to get up or not. I can't tell what time it is, but I know it has to be later than usual. Maybe I can get away with just lying here all day. Then I don't have to get up and face anyone. Why do I think that? Now I remember.

I decide I'd better go home. Yesterday, when we were crawling out of the window in the living room, I should have followed my instinct, which maybe wasn't instinct. It was probably just obvious common sense. I should have bolted down the road, and now be waking up in my own bed. Our cleaning lady would have asked me lots of questions, if she'd been there, but so what? I could have said I'm not feeling well, which is definitely true.

I stand up and look at my slept-in clothes, wrinkled, dirty and sticky. I brush my palms on them in an attempt to smooth them out, but they're beyond hope. I really need to pee, but when I go out the bedroom door and head for the bathroom, I stop. I can't go in. I feel like I've done something awful and if I go into that room with its wet towels, and its mustiness, its dirtiness, I will feel even worse. I'd like to swing the door open and scream at the bathroom, then run down the hall and scream and kick at Graham's door, then run out of the house punching the walls and breaking the lamps and throwing dishes and letting the whole family know that they're all mad. But I'm a polite guest at someone else's house, and I'll be out of here soon and I can pee in the woods on my way home. And, to make matters worse, and it makes me feel really bad, though I can hardly admit it, I want a taste of a little more.

So instead of sneaking down the stairs and out the back door of the family room, I stand at the top of the stairs and stretch my arms and yawn loudly, half expecting everyone to come running out and inquire about how I'm feeling, or why I've slept so long. At any of my old friends' houses that would definitely happen, but then again, none of the night's events would've happened at my other friends' houses. There's no reaction, so I stumble loudly down the stairs and go into the kitchen. Libby, Becca and her mother are sitting at the table, unsmiling, in silence. I walk in and look at the little clock on the stove and it says 12:15. Libby's mother takes a long sip out of her coffee mug when she sees me, without changing her expressionless face. Both Libby and Becca look pale.

"Hi," I say looking at Libby. I obviously don't want to ask her how she is feeling in front of her mother and sister. Anyway, I don't need to ask, I can tell. Everyone looks weird, like something is wrong. Maybe Libby's told her mother about getting drunk and she's mad at her, or maybe she's mad at me because I had some beer too. Or maybe they aren't thinking anything.

"We've got some chores we have to do," Libby says, standing up. I'm not sure if they are the usual chores that are supposed to get done first thing in the morning or they are new chores that have been assigned because of Libby's liquor offences. I nod, happy for the opportunity to get outside. I'm starving and there's a piece of toast sitting on the kitchen counter, and I want so much to walk over there and get it, but I can't bear the thought of heading in any direction other than out the door.

The screen door slams. Graham brushes by me, making my body flush with goose bumps. "Any coffee left?" he asks no one in particular.

"Just made some," Catherine says. He takes a mug out of the cupboard and pours himself a cup. He's wearing blue jeans and a clean white tee shirt. Libby catches me looking at him and puts her arm in mine. "Come on," she says. I turn around with her.

"I'd get out of here too, if I were you," Libby's mother says. She's speaking to us. I look at Libby, locked in my arm. She looks down and pulls me with her.

"And you," she says, her raspy voice pushed to breaking, looking at Graham, "haven't you had enough? What, you needed some new blood?" Libby yanks me with all her might and pulls me out the front door, down the steps, out onto the lawn.

She unlocks her arm from mine and grabs my hand and starts running toward the upper hayfield. We're halfway up the hill, panting for breath, when she veers into the sugarbush, over a beautiful carpet of orange and yellow leaves spread underneath us giving warm, bright light to the woods. Long after I think we ought to stop, she pulls me along, until we reach a stonewall. She lets go of my hand and sits down not on the wall, but on the ground with her back against it. Even though the leaves are damp, I sit down next to her, thinking this is her silent wish. Anyway, it's mine.

I wait for her to say something as she picks up leaves and peels the leafy part away from the stem, throwing them away around her in quick angry motions. I'm confused and there are bugs hanging in a circle over my head that I keep swatting away with my arm. I'm impatient.

"Did your mom find out about the beer?" I ask. Libby won't look at me, just shakes her head no. I feel a horrible feeling that starts at the base of my spine and threatens to take control of my shoulders. "What is it then?" Libby shrugs. "You mean you don't know or you're not telling me?" She shrugs again. I sigh. "Look, Libby," I say, trying to make the feeling go away, "I'm not feeling very well, and if it's okay with you, I think I might go home." I say "might" because it gives her a chance to say she wants me to stay. She finally looks up at me and her blue eyes are darker than usual, filled with tears. Her mouth is trembling.

"That would probably be a really good idea." Her voice, unlike the rest of her, is surprisingly steady. "So you want me to leave?" I say, feeling a little panicked. Like maybe I've done something to hurt her. I think of her mother's voice and I don't understand what's going on.

But what have I done? I've done everything right. I'd only had a little beer. I'd taken care of Libby and Becca for that matter. Maybe she didn't like the dirty clothes in the bathtub. I'd even stopped Libby from finding and maybe even smoking Graham's pot. Graham's pot. I thought of the way Libby's mother looked at me when I'd walked into the kitchen and I heard her sneering voice again, the way she'd enjoyed the distaste in her mouth for a minute, then washed it away with coffee. And that bad taste was me. She knows. Somehow she knows what Graham did to me and she's mad at me for it. She thinks I wanted to do it, that I'd agreed.

I stand up, very fast and look down at Libby. She's looking straight ahead, not at me, not at anything, digging her heel into the ground. There's too much to say to her, and I'm angry, so angry that I can't focus on anything. The forest is white and is spinning around me and my ears are ringing. I wish more than anything that she'd say something to me, or hug me or even look at me. She doesn't, so I just say, "Bye," still hoping that she'll make a move, but she keeps looking at the ground. I climb over the stonewall and into the raspberry bushes that cling to me as I push through them and head for the driveway that's out there somewhere. Maybe I'll be lucky and miss the driveway entirely and end up on the main road. I stop for a moment to pee, carefully not hitting my feet.

I climb along the side of the hill awhile, always looking down to see if I can see the road. Suddenly, it's there, quiet and welcoming. I think of staying in the trees, but I know it'll be faster to get on the driveway and walk rather than bushwhacking for a half mile or so. I climb down the bank and through the ditch up onto the road. There's more of a breeze there, and fewer bugs. My arms and feet are getting scratched and bitten, but I don't mind. I enjoy it. It makes me feel alive. If I run, I'll make it to the main road faster. And if I hear any vehicles coming, I'll flatten myself down in the ditch or run up the bank and hide behind a tree.

I begin by walking. The earth on the road feels cool and soothing to my feet that I've held with my toes curled in, as I walked over the thorns and sticks that poked up through the leaves on the forest floor. The dirt's been flattened down where the cars go, where Yellowtruck's been back and forth, endlessly, all summer. The clouds of black flies that've been following me are gone, and I feel my energy soar. I'm going to get out of here. My walking turns into a little trot and then I break into a run. The wind's whistling through my ears so loudly that it sounds like the noise I'd heard listening to an owl's wings when she dove down for a mouse in the hay field. My breathing's hard at first, but it relaxes, in time with my strides. The driveway goes down a little hill, and I know that I'm not far from where the two roads intersect. The hill's forcing more speed behind me and my arms start to windmill at my sides in happy freedom. I'll be home very soon.

"Where do you think you're going?" I don't understand how he got here without me hearing him. But I remember how he always likes to turn the engine off and coast and surprise his sisters or his friends. I slow down and I feel my shoulders hunch up in fear. I look back at Graham, but I don't say anything, I just keep walking, fast. He starts his engine up and follows beside me, and although the motor's running, he isn't in gear and he's pushing his bike along with his feet. "Get on and I'll give you a ride." Yeah, right, I think and keep walking. "Cynthia, come on. Don't act like such a little girl." That gets me because I'm sure that I'm acting quite grown up by not falling for his stupid trick.

He rolls the bike next to me, one hand on the handlebars; the other grabs my forearm, tight. "You gonna run from me?" he says sweetly. "Where are you gonna go?" He pulls me towards him. "Cynthia, get on behind me and stop taking everything so seriously."

He directs me behind him on the seat and I swing my leg over. He keeps holding one arm, but I take my other hand and hold on to the sissy bar behind the seat, just like I'd seen William do whenever he rode with Graham. Graham immediately reaches back and peels back my fingers from their grip and wraps one arm, then the other around his waist. "We're going up a hill," he explains. I raise my hands toward his chest, and he responds by pushing them below his belt buckle. There's a newer driveway that veers up to the left that goes to a house that Libby's father's been building on speculation for years, and that road goes to it. The road is always washed out, little gullies zigzagging across it with rocks and stones piled up in sloppy cairns. That's where we turn.

I'm actually glad I'm holding on to Graham because the tires are spinning and the back wheel's swaying around even with my weight on it. He maneuvers the bike well though, past yellowing berry bushes and ferns until we come to the top of the hill. Libby, Becca and I picked berries from those bushes at the very beginning of the summer. There's the house, still all plywood with a big deck that looks out to the north and the east. He pulls the bike up close to the house and quits the engine. I climb off immediately and run up the makeshift steps to the deck and I cross my arms, looking at the view.

"Amazing, huh?" he says right behind me. The yellows and golds of the autumn hills are beautiful.

"Yup," I allow him.

"You girls been inside in a while?" he asks. Once when Libby's father was here he gave us very strict orders never to go in the house, because he said there were nails jutting out of boards, and walls in the process of being sheet rocked, and so on. I'd never seen the place actively under construction, and from time to time, Libby and I'd go inside, mostly because we weren't supposed to.

"Nope," I say.

"Now's the time," he says. He pulls the front door open by grabbing an open hole where the doorknob is supposed to go, with his fingers. I follow him and it's still cold from the night before. It's pretty dark, and white electrical cord snakes out from holes in the walls where switches or fixtures will go, someday. He takes my hand and pulls me along to where Libby'd said the master bedroom is going to go and there is a big picture window. The view's beautiful and over to the west there's a front of huge dark clouds inching across the sky. The treetops below the house are thrashing about. Neither of us say anything.

Graham leads me into the bathroom that is part of what Libby calls the "master bedroom suite." It's got a big picture window too and a bath right next to it. "Reggie and I hooked up the hot water ourselves," he says proudly as he puts the plug in the tub drain. He turns the hot and cold faucets on full force. There's no pressure problem here.

I think it's a little strange that he's demonstrating with pride the water system, but I guess it's just something he's truly proud of, so I nod, affecting some interest, just being polite, I guess. As I'm looking at the faucet, he pulls off his shirt, smoothly, like he's just stretching. The water's about a third of the way up in the bathtub, and he reaches under it and pulls out two of the cleanest towels I'd seen in the family's possession. They're even folded.

"I think you'd better take a bath, Cynthia," he says in some weird sort of parental tone.

I respond automatically, as if he were my mother. "I'm not dirty," I say.

"Come on, Cynthia, you're filthy," he says, unfastening his belt and slipping off his jeans, standing there in plaid boxers this time. "It's okay," he says. "What's the difference between this and skinny-dipping?" I can't find my voice to speak. "I'll help you," he offers. He holds the bottom of my shirt with both hands and lifts it over my head, my arms responding automatically by lifting themselves skyward, like it's fine for him to be doing this. He undoes the top button of my jeans and the fly and pulls my pants down. He takes my hand and I step away from my clothes, naked, my pelvic bone seeming to protrude more than usual. I feel my hips and my ribs with my fingers and think maybe I've lost weight because I haven't eaten much for the last few days. I look up and he's looking at me. He leans forward and gives me the tiniest quick kiss on my navel and slips off his boxers. "Not to worry," he says. "Let's get warm."

I test the water with my hand and it feels great. I've wanted a bath for days, and naked in front of the picture window, I think it's just better to get in. I ease myself slowly through the water in the front of the bath. He follows right behind, sitting in the rear.

"Turn off the cold and keep the hot running," he says. I follow his instructions and paddle the warmer water back to him. It's suddenly burning my knees and feet, so I turn off the hot. It's quiet, except for the wind and drops of rain hitting the window. He's found an oval bar of soap that he's smoothing slowly up and down my spine and neck. It feels wonderful and it smells of lavender. I can't believe what I'm doing, that I'm enjoying myself. I know I'm blocking out everything that matters, but I don't care. I'm a little worried that Libby will try to look for me and she'll come here and she'll find us. She might think it was my idea, that I suggested Graham and I do this. Or even that I agreed. Thunder shakes the house and we both jump.

The rain's torrential now, running in such thick streams down the window that I can't see out of it. A few seconds later, there's a flash of lightening, and another thunderclap. Without saying anything, we both climb out of the bath. Graham laughs and I laugh too, and he shakes out one of the towels and wraps it around me. It's a big blue beautiful towel and he pulls me toward him, my arms trapped, to give me a long kiss inside my mouth. I feel like I'm six and twenty-six at the same time. He grabs up his towel and wraps it around himself like a skirt.

"You'd better get dressed," he says.

I put my jeans and underwear on first, obeying him, not looking at him, knowing that he's watching. I'm enjoying him looking, but at the same time, I don't want to be here. Again, I feel like I'm doing something very bad. I wish I'd bushwhacked through the woods to the main road.

"I guess we'll have to wait out the storm," he says. He turns away from me and pulls on his jeans and lies down on his side on the dusty floor, propping his head up with his towel. I pull on my shirt and wish that he would fall asleep and give me a second chance to escape. But I feel tired myself and roll my towel up as a pillow, like his. I lie down on the other side of the room and he doesn't stir. The voice in my head that tells me to leave is as loud as the one that tells me to stay. I feel as alone in my life as I've ever felt. My body doesn't want to move, so I wait, as he sleeps, as though I have no will of my own.

I watch as lightening flashes across the sky that's becoming dark too fast, illuminating the mountain ridges. The storm is moving away and now only large drips from the roof slide down the windowpane. Graham's completely still, in a heavy slumber, and I'm wide-awake. I think of how afraid I was of lightening storms a few months ago, even yesterday really. And now, as I lie here, I feel no fear at all. In fact, I wish the storm would come back so everything would stay the same.

Suddenly, Graham sits up and looks out the window. He doesn't turn to look at me. "Quite a storm, huh, Cynthia," he says in a way that doesn't really ask for an answer. He reaches deep into his front jeans pocket, not so easy because his pants are tight on him, and pulls out the pretty wooden matchbox that he always keeps with him, decorated in gold with a farm scene in the middle and fleur-de-lis around the border. The matches in it are wax-tipped ones from France and he is treating each one like it's a little prize, holding them daintily between his fingers. He mustn't have any other matchbooks or his lighter, because he strikes one and puts it at the end of a little glass tube, something that I've never seen him use before. He sucks in short little breaths; presumably to try to get whatever's inside it to catch, kind of like bellows in reverse. It doesn't work and the match goes out.

"Where'd the fuck my lighter go?" he says, again, to no one in particular. As I look at him, I see something in the shape of a cylinder that's making a lump in his back pocket, but I'm not about to offer him any assistance. It's a mistake to look at him for so long because he senses it and reaches around, taps his back pocket and finds what he's looking for. It's a purple plastic lighter with a picture of a marijuana leaf on it. He torches it and puts it to the end of the glass tube. He sucks the smoke in, turns around, still not looking at me, only at his pipe thing and says in gasping breaths, "Want . . . a . . . hit?" I shake my head. He blows all the smoke out in a giant cloud towards the ceiling. It smells different to me than pot usually does. It's disgusting. Kind of like burnt rubber.

"I gotta get back to the house to meet Caleb. You coming?" A direct question this time and I have no idea what to answer. I can't bear the thought of seeing Libby's mother again. If I show up with Graham, both she and Libby might think that I'd planned to meet him. I feel so guilty, but I don't understand why. I should've been stronger, stood up for myself against him. I know what I'm doing is wrong, but that I'm doing it anyway.

"Cynthia, I know something cool about the two of us that I bet you don't know," he says, breaking my thoughts. He walks over to me and picks up my hand. "Feel this," he says. He takes my palm and places it on the back of his head, just a little above the bottom of his hairline. There's a bump that sticks out, a bone, a rounded protrusion.

"And now this." He places my hand on the back of my head, in the same place as his head. There's a bump that feels like his. I'm amazed that he knows I have the bump, because I didn't even know I had it. "That means we're soul mates at the very least and that we probably knew each other in our past lives," he says, slowly. "And here we are again, in another time and space."

He moves my hand down behind my back and then the other one too so that they both are touching each other. He gently put his lips on mine and kisses me very slowly, all around my mouth. I close my eyes and find myself kissing back, enjoying him and the way he makes me feel. Despite all my guilt feelings, here I am, once again, not wanting him to stop. So, I kiss him hard on his lips, and push my chest into his, just a little.

I open my eyes and his eyes are looking down on me, like the crazy eyes of a Husky dog, my most unfavorite breed. I feel incredibly scared, but I know not to show him how I feel. I stare back into his eyes and I tell myself that I'm as wild as he is, and I keep kissing him really hard. He stops kissing me and stands back. He looks at me in a way that makes me even more afraid. "Whoa," he says, shaking his head, and I'm not sure if it's "Whoa" good or "Whoa" bad. He walks over to the sink and turns the cold faucet on and splashes water on his face and in the process, all over the floor. He picks up his drenched blue towel and carelessly pushes it around his face and chin. He throws it back down at his feet and looks at me.

"So, you like having sex with my little sister?" he asks. His chin's high, his neck arched, his eyes narrowed. Like he's asking with authority, though he really isn't asking, once again, he's just making a true statement. I can't respond and I don't want to. I have no clear idea of what he's talking about. Actually, I think he's just faking me out, that he'll start laughing and be sweet again, telling me that he's just kidding.

"Was it warm and cozy in that sleeping bag last night under the stars? Actually, excuse me, how would you know about the stars because your heads were buried." I still don't get it, whether he's joking or not, but he's talking about Libby, not Becca.

"How long have you been doing that? Was that the first time or have you been having fun with each other for a long time?"

I think of how sometimes I look at Libby when she's changing and I feel my face blush.

"Face is getting pretty red there, Cynthia," he says walking toward me. "Come on. You can tell me, what do you like best, when she touches you here?" he says pushing me with his pointer finger hard between the legs. "Or when she touches you here," he says twisting my right nipple through my shirt. The way he touches me hurts and I take the back side of my arm and my hand and push him away.

"Leave me alone," I manage. I can't believe that this is the same person I'd watched sleep, who'd played with me in the bath, the same person I'd decided not to run away from. However, he's definitely the same person who's been mean to his mother and his sisters. He's staring at me and shaking.

"Don't ever fucking push me like that again, Cynthia." I feel the emptiness of the bare walls and floor all around me and it seems much darker outside than it had only a few minutes before. I realize that I'm alone with someone I can't trust, something I've been warned about by my parents a million times, and I've arrived at that point in a way that I never could have imagined. I have to remind myself to breathe. "Do you think it's more fun being with her than me?"

"You're out of your mind," I mumble, knowing that I was out of my mind to say anything at all back to him.

"What about your little swims together, or holding hands, or playing in the leaves, or sleeping in the same bed with each other? Can't you tell that everyone knows? You two are the most despicable kind of people that live on this planet."

That's it. "I'm leaving," I say.

"Not yet," he says. He pushes me back hard enough that I fall down on the floor, but not hard enough that I can't stop my head from hitting the surface. My elbow and then forearm get the shock of my fall, and it hurts. It isn't that bad, really, but it's enough to make my eyes water and that little bit of letting go, makes me cry. Normally, part of the strategy of crying, I suppose, is to get whoever is with you to feel sorry for you, like a white flag, a truce. But in Graham's case, I should've wiped my tears away before he knew they were there. They just made him wilder.

"I thought lesbians are supposed to be tough," he says, as he sits on top of my stomach, pulling both of my arms over my head. He's able to hold both of my wrists together in his right hand. With his left hand he holds my chin so I can't move my face. "You're a fucking cry baby and a lesbian, what a beautiful combination." I close my eyes, hoping that not being able to see him will make things a little better. Maybe magically, he'll go away. It's a good thing I do, because as I do, he spits on me. That makes me feel worse than anything else he's done. I think of what I can do to him to get him off of me, either with force, which was obviously hopeless, or with words.

"When my dad gets back, I'm going to tell him about you, and you're going to get in real trouble," I cry. Graham laughs.

"The worm that's supposedly your father got me in a lot of trouble, do you know that, Cynthia? I was having a little fun at a house he had for sale that I was painting the fences for. He walked in on my friend and me, and caught us doing all the things that you and I have done Cynthia. What's he going to say when he finds out that you're really a whore who likes to have sex with me, not to mention with your girlfriend. If he finds out what you've done, Cynthia, and that you like it—'cause we both know how much you really do like it, don't we?" he whispers his hot breath somewhere in between my mouth and my ear. "If he finds out, he'll be so ashamed of you."

He lets go of my chin and sits up into a kneeling position, squeezing his thighs and groin into my sides and on the top of my stomach. He doesn't move, but just stares at me, and though his eyes look at me, I don't think he's really seeing me. He stops hanging over me, relaxes his grip and looks out the window.

"If you've made me late for Caleb, you're really going to be in trouble," he says, though his voice has lost a little of the crazy anger in it. He pushes himself up off his knees and just as he is about to step over me with his right foot, just when I've almost begun to relax with the thought he might finally be leaving, he kicks me in the ribs with the back of his heel. I scream as the pain explodes into my body. Through my crying, I hear the front door as it bangs shut and his motorcycle starts.

Finally, he's really leaving, and I know that I have to get myself out of here, fast. I have to pull myself together, stop my crying. I hear my mother hushing me in my mind. "Stop your crying, stop your crying," she always said to me when I was little. "Act like a big girl." Here's my opportunity. The pain in my left side is bad, worse when I try to take a deep breath. I wish I was a little girl so someone would wrap me up in a blanket, love me, carry me home to my bed and bring me something warm to drink, smooth my hair back, kiss me softly on my forehead.

But, I'm going to have to help myself. I'm going to have to pick my body up off the floor, walk out of here and walk home. I won't walk down the driveway. I'll walk through the woods in as straight a line as I can to the main road, and I have to do it right away because if I don't, he might come back.

I struggle to sit up, my left side just above my stomach, is killing me. My head and my arm hurt, too, but I can't think of the pain.

I walk out of the house onto the deck into almost darkness, my feet stepping into fresh puddles that have formed on the boards. I immediately feel better. So strange, just by passing through a door, my brain enters into another world. I'm surprised how much warmer it is outside. I gulp in a shallow breath of warm air. It hurts me, but it also makes me relax. I'm so glad that it's dark, because it'll be almost impossible for him to trail me, if he decides to come back.

I drag my aching side slowly to the far end of the deck, away from the driveway, thinking I might ease off it into the raspberry bushes and ferns. That way I won't make any footprints in the wet driveway that will give a hint where I'm going. Normally, I wouldn't have thought anything of jumping off it, since it's only about four feet high. But not now, I can't even stand up straight. Also, if I land in the brown crunchiness of the lady fern fronds, they're so crispy they would probably crumble and get pushed down, and if he brings a flashlight, he'll be able to see where they look different and he'll know which way I've headed. I stand up slowly and inch my way over to the steps. I go down them and decide that I'd definitely leave footprints in the dirt.

I look back underneath the deck, into the blackness and figure it out. Libby and I hid under there one day when her father wanted us to go get more nails from the nail barrel in Libby's barn, and we weren't in the mood. I step slowly off the second step from the bottom onto a ledge and stoop forward underneath the porch. I kick a beer or soda can that I can't see and the aluminum makes a cracking noise that usually I'd barely notice.

The darkness is so thick I can't see anything, only that it's lighter at the other end of the deck. What if he just moved the motorcycle, parked it in the woods and he's come back to get me? What if he's under here hiding under the smallest, darkest part of the deck where the planks meet the ledge in a tight angle, waiting? I hold my breath half-waiting for something to happen. I keep moving forward.

I reach the other end of the deck, but I don't stop, I keep stooping, fearful of the pain of standing up. I push through the brush, saplings, ferns and brambles. In the day, I would gingerly pick my way through, but not now. "Left, right, left," I pull the words from some place in my memory that I didn't know existed. They propel me forward and block out other thoughts that might stop me from getting out of here. I push hard up a hill and then it levels out and the ground clears into a stand of tall pines that are mostly quiet, except for the noise of the wind sweeping through the upper branches. There's another sound, off to the side a bit in the leaves, that's probably a chipmunk. I wish I was her, already home.

As beautiful as the woods are, I know I can't stay there. Can't be comforted here, can't pretend the quiet will last, that I'll be protected. There's too much open space between the trees, no low branches or young saplings to get lost in. Nowhere to hide, if he comes. I feel prickly beech nuts under my feet and I scratch at my scalp because it itches, a mosquito or a black fly's bitten me, and I find my hair has gathered burdocks in it, somehow. I can't remember walking through them, although that's the way it always is with burdocks.

I can't see much, but I can feel the ground dropping off underneath me quickly, so I know that I'm probably going the way I want to. At the beginning of the summer, Libby and I walked through here, looking for pine cones and acorns to make little fairy houses for Becca's birthday.

I stop because I hear something, far off, a slow popping noise. It's the engine of his motorcycle. Even though it's far away, I stand completely still, as though he might come crashing through the woods any minute. Since I'm on the other side of the hill from the house, I have no way of telling whether he's right at the new house, on its driveway, or on the main driveway. He revs the engine as loudly as he can in neutral. Now, silence fills the woods.

I know I'm so far away from him that he probably won't be able to trail me. I have a little fear that somehow I'm not walking away from where he is, that I'm circling back to the house. I did that once, when I went out for a walk in the woods near my house. I thought I'd explore through the trees, not take the old wagon road that I knew so well. Within half an hour, I was back at the same place I started.

I've been thinking with my head down, holding my ribs together and suddenly there's more light. The sky opens above me and I find myself in a field. Nothing but high grass, scrubby trees and stars. A breeze blows lightly across the saplings and me, making their dying leaves rustle and my face feel stroked, smoothed, cared for. I smile and look up at the sky that's so clear the Milky Way is completely visible. First I find Cassiopeia and Perseus, pretty much inside the cloudy trail, which means I'm facing north. The Big and Little Dipper are there too, the Little Dipper's handle shining bright with the North Star, Polaris. To the west is Hercules, strong, telling me to be strong too.

Northwest's where my house is from Libby's house, we figured it out when I first started coming here in the spring. Where I need to go now is northeast because that's where the main dirt road is. Thank God, I'm headed in the right direction. I smile once more at my friends, the stars, and walk straight ahead, out of the field and back into the woods.

I walk up against a limb that's fallen. I slowly climb over it, holding my side, the pain wrenching me as I pull my stomach over the roughness from one side to the other. It's a big white birch, with curly, powdery bark. As I drag myself over I hear the faint rumble of a car to my left. Through the trees I see headlights bouncing over the potholes towards me, the beams grayed by an autumn fog. I can't believe how close I am to the road; it's only a hundred feet away. I lie down as flat as I can, hoping I won't be seen. I lift my head a little and watch it as it passes by slowly. It isn't any car I recognize, a compact car that's not taking the bumps very well. It continues up the hill, its lights shining on the mailbox at the end of Libby's driveway. I've made it to the main road!

I have to make a decision. After what had happened when Graham suddenly appeared on the driveway, I can't walk on the road again. But with my ribs like this I can't bushwhack either. Maybe Graham's gone on to something else, maybe he's not even thinking about me anymore. He's so easily distracted. I remember one of my Dad's favorite expressions when he's talking about someone he can't get rid of. "A bad penny always turns up." So maybe Graham will suddenly appear again. I limp down a slope into a little gully and then up onto the road. It'll only be for a few seconds, just to get a feeling of what's going on.

Once again, the hard-packed dirt feels cool and smooth to the soles of my feet. I remember there's a trench running alongside the other side of the road that's pretty deep. After the town road crew graded it at the beginning of the summer, two or three cars got caught in the soft dirt at the edge and ended up down in the ditch, and they had to be pulled out by a tow truck. I can walk along the road, next to the ditch, and turn around constantly to make sure that I don't miss the sound or lights of someone coming. Besides, I won't be running like I did last time, not with my side feeling like it does. The right side of the road has the ditch, so I'll walk along there. I wander a little over to the right, just thinking about it I guess, when I remind myself to turn and look back up the road, instead of down it, to where I'm going. Just as I do, two big headlights swing out of Libby's driveway, shining against the same thick fog. I hear Yellowtruck rattle as whoever's driving goes from almost stopped to second or third gear. The dog's yapping stops for a moment as he regains his footing; I know because I've watched it before. I run to the side closest to me, the right, the side with the ditch. The road doesn't drop off though, instead, the crumbling stonewalls of the graveyard sits silently, waiting for me.

The hair is rising up on my arm and I want to run back across the road into the woods, but I know if I try it they might see me in their headlights. Besides, I can't run. There's no time left to go up or down the road in either direction, to find where the ditch begins, so I climb through a crumbling part of the wall. I let out my breath slowly and I crawl quickly from stone to stone, keeping very low, because the wall is collapsed in most places, up the gentle slope of the mossy pine needle-laden floor.

There's a row of stones in the back that must have all belonged to the same family, because they look exactly alike from a distance. I've often admired them in the daylight that falls softly on them through the pines as we pass by in Libby's station wagon. The slate they are made of is smooth, light gray, and even from the road I could see that there are elaborate curly engravings at the top of them. Next to them, there are smaller, rougher stones, which with the others form a broken wall, something I can hide behind. I feel I'll be safe there.

I wedge my way between two stones that have been placed pretty close together and put my back to one that seems like it can shelter me. A cold dampness runs up and down my back, and I pull away from it a little. The truck door squeaks open.

"Why do you always want to take a piss here?" It's Reggie's voice and no doubt he's talking to Caleb. "Fuck off," Caleb says. I can hear him peeing on the leaves.

"If you don't hurry up, she'll get home before we find her," Caleb says.

"Who the fuck cares? Let her go home."

"But she's got all his weed, and he owes us some."

Caleb's peeing is endless. "I don't know. I'd just as soon go home and drink a few beers, watch the tube."

"Come on, we'll cruise down the road to where the dirt hits blacktop and then we'll head home." There's a pause, then a last sprinkle on the leaves and the door groans shut. Yellowtruck rattles off to find whoever has made off with some pot. It seems weird to me that they're talking about a girl, because they're hardly ever with girls, but I really don't care. I'm glad they left. So this is what goes on when these guys aren't at Libby's house; bored wanderings. I can't leave now because while they're looking for whoever she is, they might find me. Huh . . . Or else, she *is* me.

I crawl back and forth a bit to keep warm and then follow the stones along to the left. Here at the end they are very rough, not tall and flat like the others. They're smaller, really just large rocks that someone liked the shape of. I touch one and it's rough, and at the same time, soft, so I know it must be made of sandstone. I like it and continue to feel along the top. When I was little I used to stop when I was on a walk after dinner with my parents and feel rocks and trees with both hands. I wasn't sure in those days what I was feeling for, it was like I just needed to. Just to understand whatever it was I was looking at better, by touching it. Now with both hands, I feel a depression in the rock. As I do, I shiver, but I keep feeling. I'm not sure, I tell myself, but I really do know, because the marks face away from the road. I use just my right pointer finger and slowly move it as the indentations form the letters D and K. There she is, buried backwards, and I'm on top of her grave.

I scramble as fast as I can to the back of the graveyard and let out my breath. My heart is pounding so loudly that it seems like it's actually inside my ears. At first I think I've scared up a grouse in the woods and she's beating her wings as a warning I'm there. It's just me though, my own scared heart. Slowly the sound ebbs away, going back to the place it should be in my body.

How is it that I came to this place? If it's like Graham said, if I really enjoyed him kissing me and holding me, being so physical with me, if I looked at Libby when she was naked, what does it mean? Am I really bad because he says all of those things are bad, which means I'm evil and that's why I've ended up in this place with another, evil girl? Maybe I shouldn't have laughed at Libby and Becca when they held their breath here. My side really hurts and though the air is cold, it feels so good on my face. I'm hot and very, very thirsty.

The only reason I know I fell asleep is that I just woke up. My clothes are damp, sticking to me, darkness is all around me; I shiver and I remember where I am and then I hear an idling engine and voices. What's going on? I listen hard and think I hear William's voice. I'm not sure though, because sometimes his voice sounds like Graham's. The truck leaves and I listen to see if I can tell whether or not they're turning into Libby's driveway, but I can't.

I wonder if it's safe for me to get up and get out of here. I figure it probably is, that they've hopefully given up looking for me, and they've decided to go on to more important things. Like making their way through a case of beer. As I stand up, the pain lowers me back to a stoop. Three miles to town, another half mile to my house. I make it down to the side of the graveyard wall, where there's an old wrought iron gate. Rather than climbing through the wall, I'm going to exit the place gracefully. I unlatch the gate and push it open. It squeaks a little and I don't like it. I want to keep the silence silent. Instead of quiet, I hear something rattling, some noise I know, but I can't quite figure out what it is. I look down the road and not far away a little light moves erratically. I stand completely still and watch. There's someone on a bicycle, trying to shift gears that won't catch right, and a clicking noise on the wheel, that try as he might, he can't fix. It has to be William.

"William?" I whisper as loudly as I can. My voice doesn't sound like it's coming from me, and I feel like I haven't spoken in a long time. The moment I speak, I freeze. Maybe it's not William at all, maybe it's Graham on William's bike or Reggie or anyone else. There's no response and the light stops moving.

"Jesus Christ, who's there?" It is William's voice. Tears sting the inside of my eyes and blur what little I can see.

"William, it's Cynthia. Is that you William?" I still can't believe it's true.

"It's me. Yes, it's me." It's William and the little light is bobbing toward me and I can see he's holding a flashlight on the handlebars. I can't move toward him, so I let him come to me. "Cynthia, what are you doing? You scared me to death!" he says laughing. I can see his whole form, his outline in the dark. It really is William. He drops his bike on the ground and continues to hold the flashlight. As he walks toward me, the point of the light bounces across the ground. He holds the light up high, shines it on my face. I squint and try to look at him. "Oh, my God, Cynthia," he says and places the flashlight on the ground. He puts his arms around me and holds me tight. He relaxes his grip for a second and then he holds me tighter than ever. He's making me feel the pain in my side even more, but I'm so happy he's here, I don't let him know I'm hurting. He kisses my forehead, like my father would, like a big brother might. A kiss that makes me cry, that makes me know that I'm finally safe. I try to fight away my tears, but I can't anymore and I sob hard, painfully. I can feel the wetness from my tears and nose soaking his shirt. I pull my face away from his chest just a little and my snot stretches with me in a long, elasticy band. I don't even care. "Can you tell me anything?" he asks. I shake my head no, my nose pressing into his chest so that I'm inadvertently wiping it on him. He laughs a little, kind laugh.

"You know, Cynthia, Caleb and Reggie must be really high tonight." It's the first time he's ever said anything about anyone being high. I mean it's always there, someone getting high, or mumbling about picking up dope at someone's house, but no one has ever actually mentioned it out loud, like it's a real thing. "I met them down the road a bit and they said they were looking for you because Graham said you'd stolen all his pot and run away. Did you turn into a stoner in the last six hours? Or is Graham up to his usual tricks of smoking weed that he owes someone else, and finding some lame excuse for how it disappeared?"

I'd guessed it right; Graham had lied to them so they'd help him go looking for me.

"You walking home?" he asks. He picks up the flashlight that's been shining into the grass as he held me. He starts to hand me the light, but then stops and directs it at my scratched feet and closely moves the beam up my body. I look down at my self as he does this and when he gets to my stomach, we can see blood all over my shirt.

"Cynthia, what happened? Did you fall or something?" I can't lift my head up to look at him, but I can shake my head "no." He holds my shoulders, steadily. "Did someone do this to you?"

I nod my head, still not looking up.

"Cynthia, tell me."

I can't tell him, because if I do I'm afraid of what will happen. Something changes in him, I can't hear him breathing, and I know that he knows. I hear him swallow.

"Graham." He states the fact. "And he said it would never hap-pen again." He pulls me close to him and he's shaking. He turns his face away from my head, but I can feel his tears as they soak through the sleeve of my shirt.

"Look, Cynthia, I'm going home to get the station wagon. I know it's there 'cuz Mom got someone else to drive her to work. I'll meet you back here. It'll probably take me fifteen or twenty min-utes. I want you to stay here. Hide yourself. Do you understand?" I nod. As I do, we hear a little popping through the exhaust pipe as the motorcycle coasts towards us. "I'm on my way."

I know that I can't get over the wall fast enough, so I run up the side of it, keeping low. I hear William on his bike, the gears rattling as he tries to shift gears. The headlight of the motorcycle shines a path across the lower corner of the graveyard as Graham stops to question his brother.

"You seen Cynthia?" he asks.

"Why would she be out here?"

"She ran away and Libby's upset." Graham knows better than to try to convince William I've stolen his pot.

"That's weird. What happened?" William, please don't confront him now. Just let me get home.

"What the fuck do you care?" Please don't fight, please go home and get the car. Please get me out of here.

"Is Mom at home?" Thank God, William's changing the subject.

"Who cares?"

"I want to take the car so I can go get some stuff for breakfast."

Good thinking, William. Whenever someone else buys the food so Graham can eat it, he won't object.

"Yeah, she's home."

"See ya," William said, the chain rattling as he leaves.

So there he is and here I am. Here we both are, in the dark, and for once, the tables are reversed. I'm aware that both of us are here and he's only aware of himself. That's the scary part though, the aware part. He knows I'm around. I feel it, but luckily, his senses are impaired. Thank God. He waits for only minutes—days to me—and he then starts off slowly down the road.

William said I should hide myself until he gets back. It's a good idea too, because I hear Graham's motorcycle, coming back up the hill. I know he can smell me. He goes right by for about thirty seconds and then I hear the engine cut out. He's decided to wait. Unless he's just getting higher. I stay completely still, aching and itching, barely daring to breathe. I'll pretend I'm one of the bushes I'm sitting next to. He might be walking over here, somehow figuring out where I am. For a moment I break my tree brain and I try to smell him, but I can't. I hear the station wagon come to a stop at the end of the driveway.

If William drives right over to where I am to pick me up, Graham will see him and I might never get home. Tears come to my eyes again, because I think I'm about to lose the only chance I have to get out of here. Please, William, don't stop here now, don't stop here now. The station wagon passes by me, by the graveyard, on down the road. My wish is granted, but I'm confused. I feel very helpless, but I have to trust that William has a plan. The silent instinctive game that Graham and I have going has officially become a triangle.

A few minutes pass by and Graham starts the motorcycle engine. He can't wait any more. Luckily, he's impatient. He knows William's up to something, that William knows where I am, and he's going to follow him. I sigh and relax a bit, letting my body shift as I hold my side.

I hear the station wagon coming back up the road. I've no idea how long it's been. Ten minutes or half an hour, I don't know. Somehow it sounds different to me. It slows down and stops. I don't move because I'm not sure what's going on. After all this time, I'm not going to run out into the middle of everything. I can see him inside, leaning across the seat. The passenger door opens.

"You can come out Cynthia." It's William's voice. He's almost shouting, his voice is so loud, not caring if anyone might be close. "Let's get you home."

I make my way slowly out of the little bushes and walk toward the car. He closes the door and I wonder if he's in a rush, if he's expecting Graham to come back any second. I push myself a little faster, then I yank open the heavy door and the yellow ceiling light flickers. William's looking straight ahead, his hands and the side of his face are smeared unevenly in dark red. It takes me a second to realize that it's blood.

"Are you okay?" I ask. As he turns his face toward me I see a huge cut on his upper lip.

"Better than I've been in a long time," he says. He picks up a gray rag that is pretty much soaked with blood and holds it on his face. "Shut the door, please," he says. I shut it and the light goes out. He shifts into gear, the only noise is our silence. I relax into the seat and watch as the headlights find our way through the fog that's gotten so thick that I can't see the trees at the side of the road. Now that I'm with William, I'm happy we have to take our time. As I watch the fog through the window, I see Graham's motorcycle in the ditch, with no Graham.

I look at William to make sure that he's seen it. I can tell he has. His eyes are wide open, so aware. But he doesn't make a move, his eyes stay right on the road. Before I can say anything, he does.

"Anyone at your house?"

"No."

The dirt changes to blacktop under the tires, the ride is smoother. Soon we are under the street lamps taking the back streets in a short cut to my house. When we get there, the light upstairs that my family always leaves on when we are away is lit. A feeble attempt to fake out would-be robbers. He pulls the car onto the driveway, alongside the back porch, and turns off the engine. I slide slowly down in my seat. I can't stay in the car, but I don't want to get out either.

"You've never invited me in, you know. All those times I've picked you up and dropped you off." I look at him to see if he really does want to come in. I push my palms onto the seat, so I'm sitting up.

"Come in if you want." He opens his door, gets out, shuts it, and comes around and opens mine. Normally, this would never happen. I'd be on the porch now, halfway in the door, waving goodbye.

I hold onto the door handle and ease myself up. My whole body has become much more sore on our short ride. William supports my elbow on my good side. We walk up the steps to the back door. The house key is kept under the mat, and my parents instructions to never let anyone see me get it out of its hiding place, go floating by in a foggy part of my mind. But I don't care about anything any more.

I unlock the door and the alarm warning sounds its steady tone, so I walk over methodically, turn on the recessed lights, and push the numbers in the control panel to turn the alarm off. Something I've done hundreds of times before. The rows of recessed lights make the stainless steel of the range, the sink, and the refrigerator gleam, perfectly polished. I turn and William looks dark and dirty next to the counter tops that are spotless, and there isn't one hanging pot that hasn't had its copper bottom scrubbed to its original condition. Our cleaning lady has been hard at work in my family's absence.

I pull the refrigerator door open and stand there, looking at all the full cartons of orange juice, yogurt, packages of smoked salmon. I don't want any of it, and I don't even bother to ask William if he does. It's not that I don't want to ask, I just don't want to talk. I push the door shut, because my bladder's aching I need to go to the bathroom so much.

As I walk by the bulletin board, I see each of our schedules neatly tacked up. Above them are pictures of my mom and my dad, but mostly of me. I look at me smiling, with my cousins at the beach, accepting my Latin prize, me playing the violin. I look hard at those smiles and then into my eyes, wondering what I was thinking when they were taken.

I walk into the little bathroom off the kitchen and turn on the light. Above the sink there's a mirror, and there I am. There's dried blood on my forehead, and little scratches, probably from walking in the woods, all over my face. My hair's tangled with burdocks, my neck thick with dirt. Even though I know it's me looking in the mirror, I don't recognize my face. As I lower my pants to pee, I slowly raise my shirt. There's blood everywhere at the bottom of my rib cage and a cut, shiney red, but it isn't bleeding anymore. I pee endlessly, past the time when I think I should've stopped, it keeps coming, but I can't feel it, I just hear it. I better go see what William's doing.

He's leaning his back on the wall across from the bathroom, kind of bouncing on it. I'm so tired. I head down the hallway, over our hand-hooked rugs, one of a farm scene with white, fluffy clouds, the other one my mother commissioned of Millie. I walk up our carpeted stairs, the softness spreading under the soles of my feet and in between my toes. By the time I reach the top, William speaks.

"Is it O.K. if I come up?"

"Sure," I say, not looking down. Something is warning me that this isn't a good idea, that once again I'm doing something I shouldn't, but I can't figure anything out any more.

I walk into my room and turn the light on. The green bedspreads on my twin beds look perfectly smooth. Each with a small, white, lacy pillow on top of the other pillows. I always throw them off every time mom carefully puts them on. I never really noticed it so clearly before, but the bedspreads match the curtains, which match the upholstery of the chair.

William pauses in the doorway. "Nice room, Cynthia," he says.

"Thanks," I say.

"You should probably wash yourself off a bit, just so if, like, somebody comes in suddenly, they won't see me here and you covered in blood."

He makes me smile. I nod, steer my body into my bathroom, and shut the door. My monogrammed towels hang in a row, two washcloths hang on top of them. I take one and turn on the hot water. The water slowly warms up, and it feels great. I don't want to look in the mirror, but I wash my face first, slowly. I lift my shirt again and tenderly wash all around my cut. Then, I walk over to the door.

"William, can you look under the pillows of the bed closest to the window and see if my pajamas are there?"

I open the door a few inches, stick out my hand, and he places them in it.

"Thanks," I say.

I quickly take off my clothes and stick them in my wicker laundry hamper. I tell myself to absolutely remember to deal with them somehow, immediately when I wake up in the morning. My pajamas are flannel, warm and cozy. Automatically, I think I should brush my teeth, but I skip it.

William is sitting on the end of my bed, where he's folded back a corner of the covers to make it look even more inviting. He stands up immediately and smiles.

"Look better already, Cynthia," he says.

things are not what they seem

I walk over to the bed and slowly sit down, then slide my legs up under the covers. I groan.

"I wonder if my side wouldn't hurt so much if I lie on my other side," I say. I shift slowly onto my right side and I feel less pain. William pulls my covers up just under my chin, then he walks over and draws the drapes shut. I close my eyes, opening them again when I hear him put my water glass on my side table. He puts two Tylenol next to it. "You want your lights left on, Cynthia?"

"Sure," I say.

I think he's going to leave and then . . .

"Cynthia, a lot has happened."

"Uh huh." I really don't want to speak.

"The thing is Cynthia, families are sometimes really messed up. When you make a friend you often don't think about or know about their family. Until you have to."

I waited to say anything. His eyes were watering, his cheeks red.

"So the thing is Cynthia," now he wasn't looking at me, "is that what Graham did to you he's been doing to Libby and Becca for a long time."

I stop breathing and the noise of the ticking grandfather clock downstairs in the living room and the rattling and hum of the refrigerator and the engines of the cars in the street all fill my ears so loudly that I can't think. But I know I am here because I am pushing my swollen bottom lip with my finger and it's puffy and it hurts. I think maybe for an instant that he means the kicking part, the part where Graham kicked me. Or does he mean what happened in Graham's bedroom?

"Do you know what I'm saying, Cynthia? He's really messed up when it comes to sex."

That clears up that, I guess.

I lie here and he sits with me for a long time. There isn't much to say, I don't want to talk about anything so awful, and everything is what it is.

91

Finally, he says, "See you," and gives me a kiss on my forehead and I feel my whole body relax. I give him a kiss in the air as he disappears out my door, pulling it not quite shut.

I am just about asleep when I open my eyes again and see that the door is open just a little more than William left it. I hold my breath, straining my ears, and Millie jumps up on my bed.

"Just let yourself in," I say. She walks up to my face and sniffs me. I open the top of my covers and she burrows in next to me, purring very loudly. I put my head under the sheet and she smells a little dusty, and I know she's been sleeping in my closet. Her fur tickles my neck and she licks my chin. I put my arm around her and pull her close to me. She puts one paw on my arm, like she always does, my little friend.

I close my eyes and hope that William pulled the outside door shut, so it's locked. And then, I begin to fall asleep, knowing that it will take forever for me to really be able to think about what has happened to me. When will I be able to speak about it? Who will really understand?

The author wishes to acknowledge each person for their unique contribution to this book—

Jamie and Mary
David Deiss
Yarrow, Dan and Elsa
Randye
Sheila
Sandy
Sonny
Pam
Michael and Tracy
Hali
James and Tresa
Deana
Charles
Penny Meyer
Ann Johnston
Jack Gantos
Patty McCormick
Stephen Scotch Marmo
Sonya H. Hall

Ken Jefferies
George Nicholson
Donna Brooks
Terry Gallowhur
The Janti
Nora
Phyllis
Charity
Dorie Friend
Sophia
Boo and Ort
George
Aunt Mary
Bill Meyer
Chris Lynch
Louise Hawes
Chick- Chuck
The Judge Family